Devil Forget Me

by

Karilyn Bentley

Demon Huntress, Book 5

This is a work of fiction. Names, characters, places, and incidents are either the product of the author's imagination or are used fictitiously, and any resemblance to actual persons living or dead, business establishments, events, or locales, is entirely coincidental.

Devil Forget Me

COPYRIGHT © 2019 by Karilyn Bentley

Cover Art by *Diana Carlile*

The Wild Rose Press, Inc.
PO Box 708
Adams Basin, NY 14410-0708
Visit us at www.thewildrosepress.com

Publishing History
First Mainstream Paranormal Edition, 2019
Print ISBN 978-1-5092-2526-2
Digital ISBN 978-1-5092-2527-9

Demon Huntress, Book 5
Published in the United States of America

She chuckles as I sip my beer. "Not nothing. I am trying to discover the identity of the demon at the Agency." She frowns. "It's not going well. I know I know who the demon is, but every time I think of its identity"—her hands move in a *poof* motion—"it vanishes."

"Yeah, I have the same problem."

A memory pops into my mind. Two memories, actually. The first was of last night's fight with Rahab. How the demon said he only had one demon left to kill in order to rule Hell. Mammon, the demon of greed. The second memory was from last week when Smythe and I went to the Agency. We ran into Chuck Tweedy, the Big Boss of the Agency, and my *justitia* couldn't stop chanting "greedy." I assumed the bracelet got its words mixed up, exchanging Tweedy for greedy. But what if there was a connection?

A dull pain hammers my head. I rub my brow. What was I thinking? We were talking about the Agency demon. Who could it be?

"You do have the same problem." Eloise touches my leg, and the headache disappears. "That's what happened to me."

"How did you know?" Eloise was blind, although I swear at times she sees fine.

"I could feel your pain." Her brow furrows. "Like a spell had been thrown at you that caused the headache. I wonder if the same thing happens when I get a headache from thinking on the demon's identity."

"Wait. You mean whenever I think about who the demon is, my thoughts trigger a spell? What does the spell do?"

Praise for Karilyn Bentley and...

DEMON LORE:
"An action packed tale of demons, guardians and magical abilities."

~*Linda Green at Fresh Fiction*

"Fantastic start to a new series."

~*Annetta Sweetko at Fresh Fiction*

DEMON KISSED:
"...the story is a snarky, fast-paced romp that kept me reading straight through the afternoon..."

~*Katie O'Sullivan at Read, Write, Repeat*

"The world is interesting and is explained well and the story is full of action, suspense and a bit of romantic drama."

~*Urban Fantasy Investigations*

DEMON CURSED:
"I also love how the author paints a picture in my mind by these spellbinding sentences."

~*Booktalk with Eileen*

DEVIL TAKE ME:
"Witty dialogue, fast pacing, captivating characters and an intriguing plot make the fourth installment of Karilyn Bentley's Demon Huntress Series a success."

~*J.C. McKenzie*

Dedication

To my wonderful husband,
who supports me in my writing career.
I love you very much.

Acknowledgements

A big thank you to J.C. McKenzie and Carrie Hamlin, beta readers extraordinaire. You make my work better!

And another thank you to J.C. for the title.

Thank you to Phyllis Middleton for the emergency responder knowledge. All mistakes are mine.

Chapter One

Local weather report for today: sunny with a chance of scattered minion parts.

I spin, my sword slicing off the minion's arm. His eyes flare, round saucers in a shocked face. What did he expect? Me to roll over and stop fighting?

Fat chance, buster. Shouldn't have hosted the demon's essence.

Minions might be super-charged on a demon's essence, but they still feel pain. And whacking off an arm causes pain.

While the minion grabs his bleeding stump and whimpers like a kicked dog, I pull back my sword for a fatal blow. One I should have administered instead of one-arming the minion.

A swing later and the whimpering stops, courtesy of the minion's head rolling across the ground. Score!

"Good job." Aidan Smythe, my guardian mage, mentor extraordinaire, and current lover, nods at the dead minion.

I draw in a deep breath, standing a little straighter. When I first became the world's newest *Justitian*—or demon huntress as I like to call me and my twelve fellow sword-sisters—I sucked at killing demons. Now, I'm Gin Crawford, super-awesome demon huntress. A feat continuing to impress me.

If only my demon-killing employer was as

impressed. Then again, in my book the Agency isn't exactly known for its intelligence.

I place my special demon and minion-killing sword, or *justitia,* against the gray mist escaping from the severed neck. While Smythe can kill a minion with his mage magic, only a *justitia* can destroy the demon's essence. Kill enough of the demon's essence and you kill the demon.

Of course, whacking off the demon's head would also get the job done, but unfortunately, the wily creatures aren't always around to kill. Good thing too. Minions are evil. Demons are a whole different level of evil. And they often come with special powers like telekinesis and teleporting, making a demon fight a load of fun.

The last of the gray mist sizzles against my *justitia* while Smythe kicks the minion's sword away from its body. Yeah, minions carry swords. Usually in a back sheath. Lacking the magic a demon possesses, they make up for it by buying and using swords in abundance.

Which makes me wonder if there is a Swords-4-Minions online retailer.

While Smythe calls in the cleanup crew I walk around the office space, checking for other minions. Since my *justitia* remains in sword form instead of changing into a bracelet, I assume another demonic presence hangs out behind a closed door.

It's not every day I track minions into an office building, up three flights of stairs, and into a space usually populated by a financial advisor. Fortunately, it's after closing hours and empty of innocent humans. Thank goodness. I hate needing to call the cleanup crew to wipe the minds of innocent bystanders. An often necessary side effect of my job.

The *snick* of a door closing draws my attention farther down the hall. My thick-soled leather boots barely make a noise on the carpet as I press myself against the wall, sneaking toward the sound.

Minion. On left. The eerie voice of the entity in the *justitia* echoes in my mind.

Until recently, the thing remained quiet, giving me no glimpse into its being. That all changed a little over a week ago when it opened up, telling me about its past. Well, sort of telling me. More like giving me visual glimpses while talking in circles. But whatever. At least it talked.

And still talks. And talks. And...

Boom!

I jump as something topples to the floor in the office on my left. Minion. Taking a deep breath, I push down on the door handle, give the door a shove, and step into the room. As I thought, a minion faces me, a bunch of you're-about-to-die written on his face. How do I know he's a minion? Most normal humans wouldn't be pointing a sword at me.

At least not in a financial advisor's office.

The minion stands about six feet tall, brown hair cut short, his clothes the latest business fashion.

"Damn *Justitian*. You're ruining my plans."

"Bummer." I waggle my fingers at him in a come-hither motion. "Come and get me." Okay, so maybe I should stop bitching about bad lines demons throw my way in the thick of a fight. I seem to be struck with the same problem.

The minion does as I ask, just like his dead friend

did earlier, without a word or taunt thrown. Unlike most demons, who continue to brag about their abilities throughout the entire damn fight.

My brain cuts to the fight, my eyes watching minute movements of the minion as he charges me. Not used to handling a sword, he swings downward, like an axe chops wood. No finesse at all. I dodge the blow, pull my sword back, and cut off his head before he turns.

The flat of my blade catches the escaping gray mist, turning it to ash. Two minions in one night. While not a record, it's pretty good for me, considering I royally fucked things up not too long ago. The outcome I'm still dealing with on an emotional level.

Tonight's fight proved I can still kill minions. That I'm worthy of the title *Justitian*. A little confidence never hurt anyone. A rush of pride warms my chest. But only for a minute. Confidence is good. Pride can get you in a lot of trouble. Something I know firsthand.

"Gin!" Smythe yells, heavy steps drawing closer.

"In here! Found another minion."

Smythe steps into the doorway, filling it with his muscular six-feet-five-inches, his black brows rising for a second as he stares at the headless minion. "Good job. Two of them. What do you think they were doing here?"

"No clue. I didn't ask." Maybe I should've been a bit more curious about what plans I ruined for the minion, but why talk with evil when you can kill it?

"I'll let the cleanup crew know another one is back here." He turns, takes a step, then turns back. "You think it has something to do with the demon in the Agency?"

I shoot him a get-real look. "Seriously? Why would it? We're in Dallas. The Agency demon is at the Agency in Boston. What would it be doing here?"

He shrugs. "Just a thought." His words remain as he walks down the hall toward the first dead minion.

The *justitia* makes a tiny *pop* noise as it transforms into a silver-linked bracelet surrounding my wrist, while I stand frozen in place, staring at where Smythe stood. Why would he think these minions had anything to do with the Agency demon? Talk about a stretch of the imagination. Or maybe I can't see the connection.

Finding the demon hiding in the Agency is on our to-do list. Right at the top. Smythe, my twin brother T, and Eloise, the Agency healer, are all working on it. With no luck. We all feel like we should know who the hell this demon is, but every time we try to puzzle it out, our thoughts scatter to other topics.

A clear clue there's some sort of spell or magic at work to keep this demon hidden.

We're on to him, or her. At least we will be. Once we can break a spell. If it is a spell. Maybe there's nothing happening.

What was I thinking about?

I glance at the dead minion as footsteps draw closer. Right. I was thinking about the dead minion and how it would suck to be on the cleanup crew. Wasn't I?

Well, it would suck to be on the cleanup crew and have to get rid of minion evidence. Better to be the sword that knocks them dead than the broom that sweeps it clean.

I step into the hall, gesturing at the office, as if the group of mages could miss a headless minion. They get to work, and I hightail it back to where Smythe stands by the front door to the suite. As I walk, my tight leather pants rub in places that shouldn't be chafed, but blood doesn't soak into them like regular pants, which is a win when you're on a fixed budget like mine. Blood is a bitch to get out of clothes.

Good thing Smythe gave me this pair of leather pants, a black, long-sleeved T-shirt, and thick-soled black ankle boots. I might look like a dominatrix minus her whip, but it saves my regular clothes from being tossed in the trash.

"We still—" Smythe starts to say, when his phone rings. He holds up a finger—as if I'm going anywhere—pulls the thing out of his pocket and puts it against his ear. "What?"

Yeah. Most people answer the phone with a hello, but not my mage.

As the tinny, undecipherable voice talks, Smythe's eyes widen, his mouth opens then closes in a tense line.

"What are you doing about it? Uh-huh…she's not ready. Yes, I know. Uh-huh. As I said, she's not ready. If you're not careful, she'll meet the same fate… What do you mean you don't have a choice? You—" He pauses, red coloring his face as white brackets frame his lips. "Fine. You're the boss, Dad. Do whatever you want." He yanks the phone away from his ear, slamming his finger against the screen to end the call.

"What happened?" Clearly something did, and it wasn't sunshine and roses either.

Smythe slips the phone into his pocket, his jaw tense. "Dad called to let us know Mila was killed by a minion."

"Mila?" I wrack my brain trying to remember who the heck Mila was and why her death was such a big deal to Smythe.

Smythe sighs. "She was one of the European *Justitians*. From Poland. They want to give the *justitia* to her sister, Tola, but Tola is too young."

"Define too young."

"Sixteen. Old enough to think she knows everything, young enough not to. That's what I was trying to tell Dad. They need to hold off giving her the *justitia* until she's twenty."

"You mean let there be one less *Justitian* in the world?"

"It's been done before. With your line when we believed it had died out. Since then, we've tried to be careful with the other lines."

"Is their line about to die?"

"No, but Tola is the last of her primary line. She has no offspring, so the direct line passed from mother to firstborn daughter dies with her. The others of her line are secondary and aren't as strong."

"What do you mean they aren't as strong? You never said anything about secondary lines not being as strong as the primary ones." After all, I was descended from a secondary line, yet wore the most powerful *justitia*. Which meant I wasn't a lightweight in the *Justitian* department.

Even if the Agency thought I was white trash.

"Direct lines tend to be stronger, we've found. You are an exception. The point is Tola shouldn't be expected to fight until she's older, but Dad wants her in there now."

I let the 'secondary lines are weak' comment slide, pursing my lips at mention of Smythe's asshat for a father, David's, insistence on forcing a teenage girl to fight against demons and minions. Even I, a newbie to the *Justitian* scene, know better than that.

"Does he want the line to die off like mine did, or what?"

"Why would he want that to happen?"

I raise a brow, silent speak for 'your dad's more crooked than a con artist.'

Smythe sighs. It wasn't until last week that he finally admitted David was hiding secrets. Until then, he refused to admit his dad did anything wrong. David might be a turd, but Smythe loved him, which meant it was hard for him to admit David had thrown in with the bad guys.

Smythe shakes his head. "What would Dad gain by letting *Justitian* lines die out?"

"Letting the demons rule earth?"

"Why would he want that?" He holds up a hand as I start to protest. "Yes, I know he seems to be pulling some shade at the Agency and definitely has a secret, or three, he doesn't want me to discover, but really, Gin, why would he want demons to rule the earth? He's not evil."

Okay, so I might disagree with him about the evil part, but arguing the point seems useless.

I shrug. "I can't help the way I feel."

He gives a short head shake coupled with an eye roll. "I know."

The cleanup crew strides to where we stand. "All done," the leader says. None of them carry the minions.

"Where are the minions?"

The leader's gaze fixates on me. "Elsewhere."

Okeydokey then. I nod.

She looks back to Smythe. "We're leaving."

"Thank you."

They nod in unison before the leader forms a portal. Two seconds later, only Smythe and I remain in the office.

"Ready?" He gestures to where the cleanup crew disappeared.

I step toward him, only to stop mid-stride as a warm brush of air blows against my back. Smythe's eyes widen at the same time the silver links of my *justitia* form into a sword with a small *pop*.

I turn, arm drawn back in readiness. My eyes widen as I stare at who stands before me.

"I knew I'd find you here, *Justitian*. Prepare to die."

Chapter Two

Rahab, the demon of Pride, the demon I lost big time to—twice—stands in front of me, a shit-eating grin covering his face. An energy ball glows in his hand. Without waiting for an answer to his bad B-movie line, he chucks the thing at me. I duck. Smythe ducks. The energy ball slams into the wall, splattering drywall bits over the just-cleaned office.

Won't the cleanup crew love to know their work was for nothing.

Taking a running step toward Rahab, I'm ready to strike his ass down. Unfortunately, the demon vanishes. Dammit! I turn, on to his disappearing act. He's performed this same trick before in a fight.

This time I'm ready when he appears between me and Smythe. My sword whistles through the air, aiming for his neck. Rahab squats. The sword passes inches over his head. He springs forward, sending me flying backward with a blast of telekinetic energy.

Before I slam into the wall, Smythe conjures an invisi-mat, which cushions my fall. Instead of busting a hole in the wall, I bounce off fluffy air and land on my feet, ready for another round.

I wish I possessed the ability to throw demons into walls with a thought. My abilities lean more toward the empathic. Or as I like to call it, my little touch-and-see problem. By touching a person skin-to-skin I can read their emotions and sometimes their thoughts.

Which is great for being a nurse and knowing what my patients in the ER feel or sometimes think, but not so hot in a demon fight.

A smug look passes across the demon's face as he leers at me. "Still no good in a fight, *Justitian*. Don't worry, I'll put you out of your misery, like I did that *Justitian* in Poland. She didn't stand a chance. Neither do you."

What is it about demons and their wanting to brag about their abilities during a fight? Why can't they shut up already?

I rush him, only to go airborne right into another invisi-mat. Thank god for my guardian mage. I'd be in a world of hurt right now without him.

I bounce off the invisible cushion, only to be slammed into the ceiling. This time Smythe doesn't get his magical mat inflated in time. Something cracks inside me. Pain splinters my thoughts. At least when I drop to the floor, cushiony depths break my fall. I can't breathe. Blood pools in my mouth and I spit it onto the carpet.

Air rushes into my battered lungs. Enough to catch my breath but not enough to take a deep inhale. I no longer feel pain, thanks to the *justitia*. A pain receptor-blocking bracelet rocks. Unfortunately, it can't do a damn thing for broken ribs and internal damage.

I need to end this fight now.

I push up to my hands and knees, staring up at Rahab. Behind the demon, a pale-faced Smythe stares wide-eyed. But only for a second. As I attempt upright, my mentor's eyes narrow, his lips move with a silent spell.

Ignoring my feeble attempt to stand, Rahab turns. Before I can blink, Smythe flies backward, crashes through a glass window into a conference room, and lands sprawled on an extra-long table.

Shit.

Maybe I got a little overly optimistic about my chances of defeating Rahab. Which is to be expected. He is the head demon of all pride demons. Being in his presence tends to give you a super-charged ego that goes way beyond self-confidence.

Been there, done that. Coming down from the pride high is a bitch.

Time to pull out the extra ability Zagan, my demon "friend," loaned me. Zagan, the demon of deceit, gave me some of his red, demonic energy to fight other demons. Sure, he has his own agenda—to become the ruler of Hell. Sure, killing Rahab would further Zagan's agenda, putting him one step closer to gaining the throne, metaphorically speaking—I have no freaking clue if Hell even has a throne. But killing Rahab means one less demon in the world.

And Smythe, not to mention me, needs a healing session STAT.

Drawing in as deep a breath as possible, I focus on tapping into the demonic energy hidden deep inside my core. The energy responds to my call, rushing outward along my limbs, driving into my sword. My *justitia* glows red with Hellfire.

Rahab's eyes widen. "Impossible."

"Better believe it, bud."

"You can't kill me. I only have one demon left before I rule Hell."

Yeah, who knew ruling Hell was so popular.

"Who's that?"

So much for bitching about demons' chatterbox tendencies during a fight. Apparently, I'm guilty of it too. Sometimes a girl needs answers. Was he referring to Zagan?

Zagan told me I needed to kill Rahab and one other demon in order for him to rule Hell. Which means there should be two demons left for Rahab to kill: mystery demon and Zagan. Not that I'm going to point his lack of math skills.

Oh wait. The demons must think Zagan is dead like the mages do. Thanks to Zagan's illusion I helped perpetrate.

Yep, I definitely have issues where the deceit demon is concerned.

"Mammon. Greed. Not that it will matter to you. I will kill you."

With those words, he lobs an energy ball at my chest. Instead of disintegrating, or flying backward, or dying immediately like he expects, I catch the thing on my sword, absorbing it into the metal.

Giving the shocked-mouthed demon my own shit-eating grin, I draw the glowing red sword back.

"Eat this, sucka." I swing the sword, releasing the red energy, now mixed with Rahab's energy ball, a lethal combination.

A stream of red light strikes the demon in the chest. He screams as his suit catches fire, as the energy probes deep into his skin. With a loud pop, Rahab explodes into fine black silt.

Catching my breath, I stare at the pile of silt. Yep, definitely glad I'm not a member of the cleanup crew.

A low moan sounds from the conference room.

Smythe. How could I be thinking about anything other than him?

I dart to where he lays sprawled on top of the conference table, my breath coming in short gasps. Damn injury. After lobbing yet another glob of blood on the carpet, I place a hand on Smythe's shoulder. He moans.

"Smythe?"

Moan.

Okay, then. A shot of panic ricochets through my limbs. I need to call Eloise now. Then the cleanup crew.

I fish around in Smythe's pocket until I find my phone. He was kind enough to carry it since my fighting clothes are skin-tight with no room for anything besides my body. Unlocking the password takes a second, and then I pull up Eloise's number and place the call. She answers on the third ring.

"Gin?"

"Smythe's hurt bad. Rahab threw him through a wall. Can you—"

She touches my shoulder. I scream and jump, sending my phone flying through the air to crash into the wall, the battery popping loose. Now my breath is really coming in short, make that super-short, gasps. My hand flutters against my chest, as if the movement can calm my racing heart. It doesn't.

"What—"

"You called. You're injured. He's worse." She drops her hand from my shoulder.

Tonight she wears a long blue skirt with a snug-fitting white blouse, her pale hair pulled into a severe bun, a look of worry etched onto her usually serene face.

Despite being blind, Eloise navigates the conference room without a problem as she steps to Smythe's head and places her palms an inch or two from his face. Blue light spreads from her hands down his body to his shit-kicker clad feet and back in waves. Smythe draws in a deep breath.

As do I. Or at least I try to.

I spit out another glob of blood. Not good. But the healer is here. Thank god.

My knees use that moment to give out and I collapse into a cushiony chair. Eloise glances at me, her sightless red eyes scanning me from head to toe as if taking in my injuries.

"I'll get you in a minute."

"Okay." A wheeze rattles my voice. Great. I don't need my nursing degree to know I'm in deep shit and the only reason I'm upright—or sort of upright; sitting counts, doesn't it?—is because the *justitia* blocks all my pain receptors and sends feel-good juice through my nervous system.

I glance out to the lobby. Shit. I need to call the cleanup crew. So much for sitting. I have to retrieve my phone. The chair squeaks as I attempt upright. Eloise turns to me.

"Sit."

"I have to call the cleanup crew and my phone is on the floor."

Her jaw tenses. "It can wait."

"There's a pile of demon silt in the lobby." I drop to my knees, upright no longer one of my abilities. Maybe Eloise has a point. Maybe I should stay put.

Fuzzy dots speckle my peripheral vision. Staying put suddenly sounds like the best option ever.

I topple to the side, landing with an *oomph* on the carpet. Breathing becomes difficult, next to impossible, short gasps failing to give my lungs the air they need.

Eloise curses. "Stay with me, Gin."

I try. But the darkness creeps in, filling my vision, eliminating my hearing, pulling me willingly into its lulling depths.

****

I float in a turquoise blue sea, wispy clouds drifting in the warm breeze above my prone body. Waves lap with a soft caress against my skin. Relaxation washes over me. A few minutes, or maybe hours, later my brain kicks in, shoving away the peaceful feeling.

I'm not on vacation, I'm being healed by Eloise.

With that thought, I sit upright in the water, the sea morphing into an office space where instead of sitting in water, I lay on the floor. Ceiling tiles come into focus, punctuated by opaque florescent lights, which were turned off. A stream of light fills the room, drifting through the shattered glass window from the lobby and hallway.

I draw in a deep breath, memory returning in a rush of image-filled emotions. Air fills my lungs. Eloise rocks. What would I do without the healer?

Probably be dead. About ten times over.

Pushing to an elbow, I glance around the room. Smythe lies on the conference room table, covered in a blue light, surrounded by chunks of shattered glass. His chest rises and falls in the rhythmic manner of deep sleep. His coloring has returned to normal. Once he wakes from the healing sleep he'll be good to go.

Voices, low and tired, soak into my awareness. I recognize Eloise but not the others. What are they discussing? Probably the way the office is trashed and all the cleanup needing to be done.

Can't clean until mage wakes. The voice of my *justitia* fills my head. *Not happy.*

You can hear them?

Me hear everything you hear.

But I've been asleep.

Still hear.

Huh. So if a tree falls in the forest with no one around, maybe it really can be heard.

Tree?

Never mind.

The entity 'never minds' right into silence.

As I start to push to my feet, I notice my phone lying on the floor where it crash-landed after Eloise scared the bejeezus out of me. I crawl to where it lays, snap the battery in place, and turn it on. The welcome screen comes up.

Woo-hoo! It works!

Using the wall as a crutch, I shove to my feet. As much as I long to touch Smythe—an almost overwhelming desire, despite seeing him surrounded by a blue healing light—I know better. Once Eloise puts a person in a healing trace, you can't touch them lest you screw up the healing. Instead, I give him a long look, reassuring myself he lives and breathes.

Staring at Smythe's dark lashes resting against his tan skin, it dawns on me the room is quiet. Too quiet. I look through the shattered glass to where the same cleanup crew from the minions' deaths stands in the lobby with Eloise. They all stare at me, concern in Eloise's gaze, irritation in the mages'.

"What?"

"How are you feeling?" Eloise steps toward me, pauses.

I close the distance between us while talking. "I'm fine. Thank you. And thank you for Smythe."

She waves a hand in dismissal. "I'm happy to help."

"Now that she's awake, can we clean the room?" Irritation laces the female mage's voice. "It takes forever to repair shattered glass."

"Do not disturb Aidan."

The mage rolls her eyes. "Of course not. We know better than that."

Eloise grabs my arm as the mages start working on the glass wall. "Where is a chair?"

I lead her to the modern gray sofa, sitting beside her. She releases her grip on my arm, clasps her hands in her lap, and stares straight ahead. As if there isn't noise coming from ten feet away where the mages reassemble the glass wall piece by piece. The repair work is fascinating to watch, yet other things occupy my mind.

"What's wrong with Smythe?"

Eloise turns to me, her red eyes meeting mine. "Concussion. Fractured skull. Bruised everything. His damage was more extensive than yours, although yours was much more acute. Your *justitia* helps with your healing."

My *justitia* rocks. Helping me heal is only one of its abilities.

"How much longer does he have left?" At her raised brow expression, I expand on my thought. "In the healing trance. How much longer does he have until we can take him home?"

"Ah. For a second there I thought you meant for me to determine his lifespan, which I can't do. As far as his healing goes, it is almost finished. He should wake by the time they finish the repairs."

I nod as I glance at the floor. No more demon remains. Or vague sulfur smell. The mages on the cleanup crew do good work. And do it fast. Despite the lead mage's warning that repairing glass takes forever, it only takes them an hour to complete. As soon as their portal closes behind them, Smythe wakes from the healing trance with a gasp.

Which has Eloise and me bolting into the conference room. He sits on the table, feet propped on a chair, hands white-knuckling the table's edge. As soon as he catches sight of me, his hands relax, tension bleeding from his stiff posture.

"You okay?"

"Yeah, you?" I step to his side. He grabs my hand.

"Did you kill Rahab?"

A smile turns my lips. "Yep. Nailed his ass."

I neglect to mention use of the red energy Zagan gave me. Smythe hates me using demonic energy despite my explaining its necessity. Demonic energy helps me kill demons. Which, any way you slice it, is a good thing.

Right?

"Good. It's about time you killed him." Smythe pulls me into a tight, one-armed hug.

I wrap both my arms around his waist and hug him for all I'm worth. Peace flows into me, a brief respite in my messed-up life.

Eloise clears her throat. "We need to leave. It's almost dawn."

She doesn't have to tell me twice. Soon this office will be filled with people unaware of the night's activities.

"I'll form a portal, Aidan."

"Thanks." Smythe pushes the chair back with his feet and slides off the table, never releasing me from his side.

Once he stands, I rest my head against his chest, breathing in his scent. A whiff of blood laces his breath. Thank god Eloise came and healed him. Otherwise he might not have made it. I've already lost him once to a misunderstanding. I refuse to lose him to death.

In the few months I've known him, Aidan Smythe has wormed his way into my bruised heart. Not that he's healed it or me—I'm not so sappy and love-struck as to say, or think, anything along those lines—but he's completed me in a way I never thought possible. I'm a better person with him by my side.

Okay, maybe I am being a sappy fool. Whatever. A near death experience tends to do that to a person.

Smythe leads me to the portal and together we step into its chilly depths.

Chapter Three

The portal drops us into my dark living room. My twin brother and current roommate, T, should be asleep. A quick check along our telepathic link places him in his bedroom dreaming, oblivious to our arrival, and more importantly, oblivious to my fight with Rahab. T takes issue with me killing demons and minions. He's afraid I might get hurt. So he decided to use his ghost talking abilities to help me fight the good fight.

Now, I'm scared he might get hurt. Which means it's better if I sneak off on a demonic killing spree and tell him about it in the morning.

Smythe flips on the light. I slap a hand over my eyes to ward off the sudden brightness. Ouch.

"Is T here?" Eloise asks, not flinching at the light.

Yep, she likes my twin. He returns the sentiment ten-fold. One of these days they might actually act on those feelings and do something besides hold hands.

"He's asleep."

Expectation vanishes from her face. "Oh. In that case, I should be going."

"Thank you again." I give her a hug.

"Yeah, thank you." Smythe also hugs the healer.

Eloise smiles. "Always happy to help. Does T work today?"

My mouth opens, closes. Does he? "What day is it?"

"Friday." Eloise again to the rescue.

"Sorry. Yes, he does. Why?"

"We need to go over plans. We haven't had success contacting the ghost or ghosts who roam the Agency."

Too many entities besides humans inhabiting the building. Something we're working on solving.

Eloise needs T to talk to the ghosts haunting the Agency in hopes they can give us a hint as to the identity of the demon living there. T once saw a ghost at the Agency but was afraid—not that he'd use that particular term—of talking to it. Or telling Eloise he saw one.

He has history with the see-through buggers. When we were teens, an evil ghost helped him—make that us—commit a crime to escape our abusive father. Needless to say, having the ghost of a serial killer talk to him freaked T out, the end result being he refused for years to attempt talking to any ghost.

Until I became a *Justitian* and he saw me battling demons and minions. Then he decided to get over his fear of the spirit world and use his abilities to help me fight.

While I'm glad he's working through his fears, I'm not so glad he's training to fight by my side. What if he gets hurt?

Smythe's voice snaps me back to the here-and-now. "He's usually home by six in the evening. Why don't you come over and we can eat dinner and talk about it?"

"I'll see you then." Eloise forms a portal and vanishes inside its deceivingly warm depths.

"Looks like we have a dinner guest." Smythe

wraps an arm around my shoulder as he leads me into the kitchen.

I flip the living room light off. We. I like the way the word rolls off his tongue. I like the implication behind it. We. Not me. Not him. We. Together.

At the same time, I'm afraid of what 'we' can mean.

My scalp prickles as dampness coats my palms. *Nope. Stop it, Gin. Obsessing on the matter will do nothing but fuck it up.*

Instead of over-thinking things, I smile at Smythe as he leads me through the kitchen and into my bedroom.

"Guests are good. Besides, we do need to meet up. We haven't had a planning session since last week."

He kicks the door shut as soon as we step into the room. His lips brush against mine.

"Whatcha say we take a shower before going to bed?"

Considering I'm covered in demon blood, his idea sounds like a winner.

****

A movement against my wrist wakes me from a deep sleep. Light streams between the blinds, a not so subtle hint dawn was hours ago. A heavy arm drapes across my waist. Smythe's rhythmic breathing drifts into my ear, lulling me to sleep. I close my eyes.

My *justitia* jiggles again, harder this time.

Friend here! Wake up!

I sigh. So much for relaxing after a hard night's fighting.

Was easy night fighting. Now friend here. Hurry!

How I long for the days before the *justitia* started

speaking to me.

Liar. You no long. Hurry. Friend here.

I know, give me a second. I know who its friend is and am not so sure I want to see Zagan, the demon of deceit, right now. Maybe later.

A sharp sting shoots through my limbs, courtesy of my overeager bracelet. I jump. Smythe mumbles. He rolls over, giving me the room I need to get out of the warm bed.

Double dog dammit.

Fine. I'm going.

Hurry!

Yeah, yeah, yeah. I yawn, stretch, then shuffle to where my robe drapes across the chair. The morning after a long night is not my friend. Unfortunately for me, the entity in my bracelet won't let me sleep until I take it to visit its friend.

Who would've thought a *justitia* could have a demon as a friend? Clearly not the Agency. They refuse to believe me.

Considering they have secrets of their own, that might be a good thing.

After yanking the robe around my body, I tie the sash. A quick glance to my bedside clock shows it's ten in the morning, long past the time T left for work.

The thought of work turns my stomach into a hard knot. If I hadn't been put on administrative leave for missing too many days in my efforts to rid the world of minions and demons, I'd be at Blue Forest Emergency Department now. I love my job as an ER nurse. Unfortunately, my demon huntress gig gets in the way of twelve-hour shifts. No big surprise.

I yawn. I'm pretty sure I need several more hours

of z's to grab my eight hours of sleep for the night. Or day as the case may be.

At the moment, I need to shove aside the wave of tiredness as well as thoughts about my on-hold nursing career and focus on the upcoming talk with Zagan.

I open the bedroom door, step through, and close it with a small snick. Drawing in a deep breath I walk down the short hall into the kitchen.

Zagan stands in front of the sink, dressed in a white button-down shirt and black pants, staring out the window at the neighbor's house. Scoping out the place? Maybe I should take a greater interest in my neighbors if a demon watches them.

At my approach, he turns. A grin curves his full lips. "Hello, *Justitian*. You look...tired."

"Thanks. It's nice to see you too." I yawn. Silver links jitter against my skin, the entity's way of saying 'happy to see you'. I shake my wrist. "My *justitia* says hi."

At the word '*justitia*' his nose wrinkles.

"That is not her name." He speaks a name unpronounceable on human lips. The bracelet's name in Demonese. A millennium ago, Zagan crafted the *justitias* for demonic purposes, using souls of gnome-like creatures and grafting them into human women.

Which turned out to be a mistake. The women learned a spell that broke their bond to the demons, allowing them to escape into the world, using the demons' own weapon against them. The women met a group of mages and *voila* the Agency was born. At least that's my version of the story. The Agency lost the history lesson some time ago. As in, when asked, they have no idea how they started, or where the bracelets came from, all they know is the *justitias* kill demons and minions. With an answer like that, why do they need to know the question?

Yeah, in my opinion the whole organization is more corrupt than the demon standing before me.

The demon who looks like he expects an answer. Did he ask a question?

"What?"

"Try to say her name."

"I can't and you know it."

He sighs. "Humans."

"Yeah, yeah. To what do I owe the privilege? I had a long night."

His eyes narrow for a second, as if he finds my attitude off-putting. Whatever. If he wanted me all happy and perky, he shouldn't have portalled into my house when I was asleep. Although in all fairness, most people are awake at ten in the morning.

Not that I feel like being fair at the moment. I feel like going back to sleep.

"The long night is why I am here. I owe you thanks."

Now that's something you don't hear every day. A demon telling you thanks. On the other hand, I'm not so sure that's a good thing.

"Thanks?"

One black brow raises, a curious expression crossing his olive-toned face. "You are tired."

"Way to be observant. We got back at dawn. I need more sleep."

"I will give you the sleep you crave. After I tell you my thanks." He steps closer, one hand outstretched as if to touch my cheek. An inch away from my skin, he drops his hand, apparently remembering my empath abilities threaten to hemorrhage my brain when he touches me skin-on-skin. At least he remembered. Eloise would not appreciate being called for a preventable injury.

His black soulless gaze meets mine as his fingers touch the center of my sternum, below where the lapels of my robe cross.

"I owe you thanks for disposing of my enemy. You will need my energy for your last fight. For my last enemy. Use it well."

A shiver courses through my limbs, sinking into my core as he fills me with demonic energy. An orgasmic rush spreads through my limbs. My knees buckle, and I drop to the floor. When my sight finally returns, Zagan is gone.

I should be happy he's disappeared. I'm not. I no longer question what that means about me. Some things are better left undisturbed.

Chapter Four

When I wake the second time, after falling back asleep beside Smythe's warm body, I decide to come clean with him about Zagan's visit, along with the demon's visit a week ago that I've never admitted. After I take another shower. Because, you can never have enough showers with a sexy man.

Not to mention Smythe hates it when I talk to Zagan. Okay, maybe that's the real reason I've put off admitting to the demon's visits. Smythe might decide not to hop in the shower with me once he realizes I've agreed to help the demon win Hell's throne. So, shower first, confession time later.

After a slow, hot shower, we dress and go into the kitchen. Smythe pulls out steaks to defrost while I make coffee.

"Coffee at two in the afternoon?" Smythe shakes his head.

"Shut it. I don't want to hear it. As far as my body is concerned, it's seven AM." I flip the switch on the coffeemaker to the ON position then lean against the sink with my arms crossed, giving him a glare.

His lips twitch. I return the grin. I'm addicted to coffee. Smythe is learning to live with my need for caffeine. He'll give up on the teasing eventually.

Giving me one more head shake complete with a grin, he moves on to more important topics.

"Eloise will be here at six. Does T know she's coming over?"

I shoot him a 'get real' expression. "And when would I have had time to talk to T?"

"I thought I heard you talking to someone in the middle of the night."

"It wasn't the middle of the night. It was ten in the morning." The words pop out before my brain weighs in. Dammit. I hadn't meant to spill the Zagan beans yet. Oh well. Since the proverbial cat was already out of the bag, I might as well move forward with my soon-to-be ass-chewing session. Besides, the longer I hide the conversation, the worse it will be for our relationship. Trust is everything to Smythe and his trust in me is already a little shaky due to past issues with the demon of deceit. So why does it feel like I'm ratting out my best friend?

I take a deep breath, releasing my words in a rush. "It wasn't T. It was Zagan."

A palpable wave of anger washes over me as Smythe narrows his gaze. His jaw tightens.

"I thought he'd left you alone."

I stare at the floor as I press against the counter. Stupid reaction. Grow a pair, Gin. I raise my gaze to meet his. "Yeah, about that." I pause.

"Gin." His tone holds enough irritation to make me cringe.

I draw in a deep breath. I'm a big girl. Big girls don't shirk responsibilities no matter what the consequences. I need to tell Smythe and admit the bargain I struck with Zagan. I need to get this over with now.

"He visited the night we defeated Perdix." Perdix,

the demon of despair, used telepathy to sway his victims into committing suicide in order for him to gain a power rush. With the help of T and a group of ghosts, I killed the bastard.

"He what?"

I lick my lips. "I'm sorry. I should've told you. I meant to tell you. But I knew you'd be mad." Even to my ears, those words sound like a half-assed excuse.

Probably because they are a half-assed excuse.

He draws in a deep breath. Opens his mouth. Closes it, his lips pressing together in a white line of ire. "You shouldn't be consorting with a demon. Especially that demon. What if the more you are around him, the more likely you are to truly become his servant?"

The servant thing is a possibility. When we first met, I accidentally gave Zagan crackers to eat and a bit of my blood. In exchange, and without my knowledge, Zagan marked me as his with a small tattoo behind my left ear, right below my hairline. How was I supposed to know giving him food and blood meant I became his servant? The demon was hungry, and my thought was better crackers than me.

So much for thinking.

And yet, nothing came of it. Sure, I've helped Zagan fool the Agency into thinking I killed him, but I admitted it to Smythe. After Smythe called me out on it. And Zagan gives me demon-killing red energy. One less demon in the world is a good thing, right? Besides, I don't do everything Zagan asks.

Therefore, I'm not his servant.

I hope.

Doubts I refuse to tell Smythe. No sense in

worrying the mage more than he already is.

"He doesn't control me. He asks. Not commands. And I can always say no."

Smythe crosses his arms. "What did he ask now?"

"Nothing this morning, but after Perdix was killed he wanted help."

"Dammit, Gin. I told you not to help a demon."

"This is different. He wants me to kill certain demons in order for him to ascend to the throne and rule Hell." Zagan didn't use those exact words, the ascend to the throne part, but it makes good imagery so I'm going with it.

Smythe blinks. "Come again?"

"Zagan wants to rule Hell. In order to do so, he needs certain demons gone. Like Perdix and Rahab. He said there's one demon left and that's the worst one of all."

"And you agreed to this?" Both brows rise.

I shrug. "Come on, Smythe. I'm killing off demons. Fewer demons is a good thing. It's what I do anyway."

"And what do you get in exchange for helping him become the ruler of Hell?"

"He wants the demon leaders eliminated. Once they are gone, all that are left are the lesser demons, the ones who aren't as strong. This means that us *Justitians* aren't fighting the strongest demons, we're fighting weaklings. We'll win more often. That's a good thing. How can you see it any other way?"

Two seconds pass as he stares at me before answering in a tone of voice normally reserved for stubborn idiots. "Minions are your primary targets, not demons. Demons don't often come to the earth. How does it help you to fight weaker demons if it's usually the minions you kill?"

"We can spend more time fighting the minions since we won't have to worry about dying fighting a demon."

He pauses. "Do you really believe that?"

His get-real stare abrades my already frayed nerves.

"Yes! How can you not? I help him, he helps us."

"What I don't understand is why you are so insistent about helping him in the first place. No matter what he promises, he's a demon. More specifically, the demon of deceit and lies. Think about that for a moment. He. Fucking. Lies. All the fucking time." Smythe's voice rises.

My temper meets his and ups it one, expanding into an entity with no thought, no reason, only pure emotion. He needs to understand. He needs to see why I have to help Zagan.

"So what? He's always been there for me. Always. Even when we were kids. How do you think T and me eluded the cops for so long? Because Zagan helped me tell lies so no one would know I killed my father. He helped me. How can I not help him?"

By the way Smythe's eyes widen as his mouth gaps, I realize I said the one thing I swore never to speak of to another human besides T. How did that happen? How could I spill my deepest, darkest secret, the secret I swore to take to my grave?

And did Zagan really help me when I was a teen? Those words spat out of my mouth without thought, but I realized them for the truth. A memory of me lying to the cops slams into my mind.

My surprise at how easily they believed me, how our story for our father's disappearance rolled off my tongue, how my face mustn't have shown deceit. No wonder the demon stalked me. No wonder he claimed he knew me long before I became a *Justitian*. No wonder he marked me as his servant.

I've been his for years.

My expression mirrors Smythe's, all shock and horror. To hell with how long Zagan's known me. Smythe is all that matters. What will he think of me now? Where do we go from here? How the hell can I retract my patricide admission? Do I ignore it? Do I grab myself a cup of coffee like nothing happened? More importantly, what's he going to do about it? The statute of limitations on murder in Texas never expires.

Instead of condemning me, he takes a step forward, wrapping me in his arms, pulling me into a tight hug.

"I thought you'd never admit to killing him." His voice brushes against my ear.

I freeze. Surprise mingled with relief runs through my veins. He's not going to turn me in to the cops. Is he?

I pull back. He releases me.

"No, I am not."

He read my mind again. I hate it when he does that. But more important things take priority right now than calling him out on it.

"You're not surprised."

He shakes his head. "I saw some of it in your mind. Back when we first started working together before you could block me."

My eyes widen. "I can block you?"

"Occasionally." His grin fades. "Why did you do

33

it? Abuse?"

I blink at his insight. A chill passes through me, riding on a wave of awful memories. My gaze drops to the ground.

"Our father was horrid. The things he did…"

"I'm sorry." Smythe pauses, a wrinkle forming between his brows. "How did you get rid of the body?"

I turn, running a hand through my hair as I stare at the coffeemaker. Steaming coffee fills the pot, a plea for me to drink, to swallow away my worries.

But Smythe wants an answer. And deep in my soul I want to tell him, to wash my secrets away, to admit my guilt.

What would T say when he found out I told Smythe? It is his secret too. A tinge of remorse wafts through me. The part of me used to hiding cries out for me to keep silent. I can't. I want to tell Smythe. I want to admit everything to him.

Even if it means T will freak when he learns what I've done.

I swallow, keeping my gaze steady on the pot of steaming black liquid caffeine. I white-knuckle the counter in an effort to steady my voice.

"We've kept it hidden for years."

"I know. I looked at the police report."

Surprise smacks me and I blink it away. I shouldn't be surprised. Once Smythe gets an idea, he's like a dog with a bone, gnawing at it until the marrow pops free. Yet, the fact he discovered something I thought I kept hidden so well shocks the hell out of me. After a couple of deep breaths, curiosity takes over. I face him. "And?"

"They closed the case after talking to your mom

and his coworkers. He'd talked of leaving so they assumed he left."

"Yeah." I nod, knowing this already. "Mom was glad the beatings stopped."

I grab my extra-large mug out of the cabinet and apply a liberal dose of coffee to its insides. After this discussion I need it. Hell, after this discussion, I want a drink of the hard liquor variety, but after my slippage a couple of weeks ago, hard liquor is the last thing I need.

"She made up him leaving?" His eyes widen, narrow in thought. "I can see that, but how about his friends? Pretty lucky break."

"I have no idea about that." I shrug. "Maybe he really was talking of leaving. It wouldn't have changed the outcome." I take a hot sip. "It's why T refused to talk to ghosts for so long."

"What do you mean?"

"An evil ghost told him how to do it."

His forehead furrows. "I thought you did it."

"I was the contingency plan. I did it when T couldn't."

It. An innocuous word sounding much smaller than the reality of the situation. A placeholder word for a truly momentous event. A way of making things sound better than what they truly were.

It.

The changing point in my life.

Smythe stares for a blink too long as if waiting for me to elaborate. I don't.

"A ghost instructed you?"

Words tumble from my lips. I started this conversation. I might as well finish. "The ghost of a serial killer. Not only did it give us an idea on how to kill the bastard, but it told T to bury the body in a freshly dug grave. We lived down the street from a graveyard. Wrapped the body in trash bags, stuck it in the trunk of our father's car, grabbed a shovel, and found a grave. No one looked for him there. It wasn't like he had a marker. Well, he did, but not with his name on it."

"Sneaky."

I shrug. "It did the trick."

"I'm amazed you kept it a secret for so long. That the police didn't come back around."

"Oh, they did." A small frisson of fear shakes my spine. Fear of getting caught continues to haunt me despite the passage of years. "But we got rid of a good deal of his personal effects and a suitcase and his car. Made it look like he really did leave."

Smythe opens and closes his mouth, as if he has another question. *How did you get rid of his car*, drifts through my mind, but he doesn't voice that thought, so I keep the answer to myself.

"I'm sorry you had to go through that." He touches my shoulder. I lean into his touch, but only for a second, only long enough for relief to slide through me.

He wasn't going to nark us out.

"Yeah." I take another sip of tongue-burning coffee. The burn felt good. Cleansing.

Smythe clears his throat. Drops his hand. "Your past doesn't excuse your relationship with Zagan. It helps explain things but doesn't excuse it. You need to stop talking to the demon."

Ah. Thank god he returned to the original topic of our conversation. I can handle having him chew out my ass much better than a forage into the depths of my soul. Tension flows from my shoulders. Discussing Zagan is a relief, a well-traveled path of disagreement.

"I can't."

His jaw tenses. "Because your *justitia* is his friend?"

"And I want to help him win. It's going to help us in the long run. Think about it. No more calls that a *Justitian* has died by a demon's hand. Wouldn't that be nice?"

"Sure it would. I'm not saying it wouldn't be. But the end result doesn't excuse the means to get there."

A burst of anger tingles along my nerves, but I'm so relieved he's not going to turn me in to the cops, the anger fails to grow. Which doesn't mean I give up on Smythe being swayed to see things my way.

"I'm not going to stop talking to Zagan. Besides never seeing him again, which isn't my choice since he pops into my house at will, what would you have me do?"

Smythe runs a hand through his hair and releases a deep breath. I keep quiet, sipping my coffee, while various thoughts dance across his face as he tries to determine the best response.

His gaze narrows on me. A sliver of unease slides down my spine.

"He has control over you."

At my protest, Smythe holds up a hand.

"Hear me out. You might not think he controls you and he definitely doesn't control you like a demon normally controls a marked human servant—"

"I am not his servant."

He glares at my interruption. "He marked you as one. It doesn't seem to work on you like it does other humans who have been marked. But you still want to do what he asks."

"That's because we have a history. He's helped me fight demons. And my *justitia* was his well-loved servant millennia ago. And he makes good points."

Smythe gives me another of his famous get-real stares. This time I return the look. "As I was trying to say, you can't get away from Zagan's thrall until you get rid of his mark."

"First off, I'm not under his thrall. Second, how the hell do you expect me to remove his mark? Laser tattoo removal is not getting rid of that thing." I point to the mark on my neck. Does Smythe really expect me to erase Zagan's mark? Wouldn't I have already done that if I could? On the other hand, my mage has a point. The only way I can convince him Zagan has no control over me is to remove the demon's servant mark.

"I can research it."

"Haven't you already done that? Like when he first marked me?"

Red tinges Smythe's cheeks. "I couldn't find anything. But I didn't search all the ancient scrolls in the library. Something is bound to be in one of those."

I roll my eyes. "Go on and admit it. There isn't anything about removing a demon's mark because the human servant was always killed."

"There's a first time for everything."

Smythe. The unending optimist.

"Okay. Whatever. I do want this mark off." Not so much because I agree with Smythe that Zagan holds me under his thrall. Or that I am the demon's servant. I'm not on either count. But walking around with a demonic mark tattooed into my flesh doesn't exactly put me in my happy place. If Smythe can discover a way to make me mark-free, I'm down with it.

"Good to know we agree on something."

I grin. "We agree on a lot of things." I set my mug on the counter and pull him into an embrace.

His stiff posture relaxes after a moment. His arms wrap around mine as he kisses me. Too soon the kiss ends, and he steps away.

"You'll be okay. Zagan won't enthrall you and turn you into his servant for real. Whatever it takes I'll make sure of it."

A promise I hope he can keep.

Chapter Five

By the time T gets home from work and Eloise arrives via portal in the living room, Smythe has shown off his expertise at grilling steaks. The aroma of chargrilled meat fills the backyard with nose-sniffing goodness. Perfect Texas early November weather, high 60s and a low evening sun, makes standing outside on the patio watching the steaks sizzle on the grill a pleasant experience. Even more pleasant? Watching Smythe. Yummy.

T opens the back door holding two beers. His grin matches my own when he sees me. Taller than me by several inches, he nonetheless looks like a shaved-bald male version of myself. He catches the door with his foot as Eloise grabs his arm, letting him escort her down the few stairs to where we stand on the small patio. He hands me one of the beers.

"Thanks." I give him and Eloise a hug, then take a long sip of the beer. Good thing beer isn't the hard stuff and therefore doesn't count as a drink to avoid. I'm not sure I could live without it.

T heads toward Smythe for some male bonding. Or to drool on the food.

Eloise smiles at me, brushing a lock of long, pale white hair off her shoulder. She usually wears her hair back in a bun or braid, not loose, but I like the relaxed look on her. I pat her arm, leading her to the outdoor furniture I bought on sale at the local home goods store. She arranges her long blue patterned skirt as she sits.

"What did you get up to today?" What does an Agency healer do all day? Heal people? Are there a lot of mages and *Justitians* hurt every day?

"A little of this. A little of that." She shrugs.

"In other words, nothing."

She chuckles as I sip my beer. "Not nothing. I am trying to discover the identity of the demon at the Agency." She frowns. "It's not going well. I know I know who the demon is, but every time I think of its identity"—her hands move in a *poof* motion—"it vanishes."

"Yeah, I have the same problem."

A memory pops into my mind. Two memories, actually. The first was of last night's fight with Rahab. How the demon said he only had one demon left to kill in order to rule Hell. Mammon, the demon of greed. The second memory was from last week when Smythe and I went to the Agency. We ran into Chuck Tweedy, the Big Boss of the Agency, and my *justitia* couldn't stop chanting "greedy." I assumed the bracelet got its words mixed up, exchanging Tweedy for greedy. But what if there was a connection?

A dull pain hammers my head. I rub my brow. What was I thinking? We were talking about the Agency demon. Who could it be?

"You do have the same problem." Eloise touches my leg and the headache disappears. "That's what happened to me."

"How did you know?" Eloise was blind, although I swear at times she sees fine.

"I could feel your pain." Her brow furrows. "Like a

spell had been thrown at you that caused the headache. I wonder if the same thing happens when I get a headache from thinking on the demon's identity."

"Wait. You mean whenever I think about who the demon is, my thoughts trigger a spell? What does the spell do?"

Smythe turns to look at me. "Spell? What are you two talking about?"

"We were discussing trying to learn the identity of the demon at the Agency when Gin got a headache. It feels the same as when a spell is thrown to cause pain." Eloise answers Smythe while staring at me as if by doing so she could learn what spell gave me a headache.

More power to her.

Smythe's gaze grows distant, lost in thought. T steps beside him, looking between the three of us with a puzzled expression before shrugging and taking a sip of beer.

After a long moment, Smythe presses a hand against his forehead and winces. "You're right. I do get a headache when thinking about the demon's identity. It seems like the demon cast a spell to protect its identity."

"That's one hell of a spell." I look at our resident mage and spellcaster extraordinaire. "How would you even cast something like that?"

Smythe shrugs, brows drawn tight. "I've never heard of a spell able to work on thoughts without the caster being present."

"It's an extremely difficult spell." Eloise taps her fingers against her thigh. "If a spell has been cast, it would explain a lot. Like how the demon has managed to hide for so many years."

Eloise first noticed a demon living at the Agency before any of the rest of us were born. Yep, despite looking mid-thirties, she's who-knows-how old, and was alive around the turn of the last century. According to Smythe, healers hold their age well, but still.

"They'd have to recast the spell a lot."

Eloise shakes her head at Smythe. "No, I don't believe they would. If a demon was powerful enough, they could use blood magic and the spell would last years."

"How would you know?"

A smile creeps over her lips, a smile hinting at secrets. "There's a lot about me you don't know, Aidan. Suffice it to say, I should have realized a spell had been cast. I should have realized it years ago when I first had suspicions."

T pats her shoulder. "Don't feel bad. If a demon cast a spell, then you forgot what you should've known. Blame the demon, not yourself."

"If the steaks are done, can we carry this discussion inside?" I was hungry, and we could discuss this indoors over dinner.

Smythe shrugs, picks up the tongs, and puts the steaks on a plate. T places Eloise's hand in the crook of his elbow while I turn off the grill. Following Smythe, we all go inside. I pull the baked potatoes out of the oven and plop them on a plate. Everyone takes their seats while I remove the salad from the fridge and put it on the table. It's eating time.

The steaks are tender and juicy, unlike the conversation, which is hard, dry, and marbled with confusion.

"How do you know a blood-driven memory spell, Eloise?" Smythe stares at the healer. That's my mentor—never gives up, never lets a conversation point drop. Since his tenacity isn't directed at me, I keep my mouth shut. Besides, I really want to know the answer.

As much as I like Eloise, she cloaks herself in an aura of secrecy.

Eloise pops a piece of steak in her mouth, chewing with the speed of a person who hopes to avoid answering. Good luck with that one.

"Do we have to get into this now? We should be focusing on the demon, not me."

"Yes." Smythe leans back in his chair, crosses his arms, and gives her his 'spill it' glare. Not that she notices his look. Although red tinges her cheeks as if she can see his expression.

She told me once if she knows a person really well she can see out of their eyes. Not sharp and clear, but enough to know shapes and object locations. Maybe she really could see the look on Smythe's face.

Before she can answer, T clears his throat. "She has a point. What difference does it make?"

Smythe turns his glare to my twin. And there went the cap on the testosterone level in the room. I can practically feel the male aggression.

Considering his expression, his voice remains steady and calm. "That's not a spell we learned, and I've gone through the highest level of mage training there is."

Mage training 401? Who knew that existed? Although I should've realized. It's not like a mage wakes up one morning knowing every spell in the book. Or scrolls, as the case may be.

Smythe continues, interrupting T's "So what." "Not to say I read everything in the library, but a spell using blood magic to extend memory loss when the caster is not present...Well, that's not in any of the books I saw."

Translation: if Smythe didn't read it, then it was either buried in a bunch of old scrolls in a dusty, cobwebbed corner of the library or it didn't exist at the Agency.

My bet is on it not existing at the Agency. I know Smythe. The man is thorough when it comes to researching. He'll leave no ancient scroll unread in his search for answers.

Eloise sets her fork down and stares at her plate as if it could respond. She holds out a hand to silence T when he jumps to her defense.

"I don't want to tell you. But I suppose trust would be an issue if I did not."

Smythe nods. Eloise continues after a deep breath and a pause.

"I used to live with a demon."

We all stare at her as if she sprouted a set of horns. Which in a way she did.

T recovers first, jumping to the rescue of his crush. "I'm sure it's not as bad as it seems."

I'm sure it's worse. Why would anyone voluntarily live with a demon? Provided it was voluntary. A shudder shimmies through my limbs.

"Did they kidnap you?"

She looks at me. "No. I was...disowned by my...family. I thought living with demons would be a form of revenge." Her gaze lowers. "It didn't work out like I intended."

I can imagine. Not the route I'd go. On second thought, growing up I'd have done anything to get away from my father, even if it meant living with demons. How bad was Eloise's family?

Smythe's eyes widen as red tints his cheeks. "I'm sorry. I didn't realize that was the reason. I mean, I thought you learned a high-level spell from someone at the Agency, not the demons. Living with them must have been hard on you."

Her head jerks up as her red, sightless eyes glare at him. "Hard? You have no idea how hard my life was."

"Okay, okay." T holds out his hands, in a 'stop right there' motion. "We can agree everyone here had a shitty childhood. Except maybe you." He glances at Smythe, who gives a half-shrug. "No one wants to relive their past so let's move on. How do we defeat this demon?"

"Defeating it is easy." I smile. "Finding out who it is, is the hard part."

Eloise draws in a noisy breath through her nose, blowing it out through her mouth as an anger release. Smythe's 'I can't believe I asked that' expression eases back to his normal look, with the exception of a slight red hue covering his face.

"We can try the Agency again, T." Eloise turns to my twin. "Maybe you can talk to a ghost this time. If not, we can study more ghost talker lore."

"Okay." T nods. "I can call in tomorrow."

"What?" I raise a brow at him. "You've called in twice already over the last week. Any more and they'll can your ass."

"Nah. Don't get your panties in a wad, sis. They're not gonna let me go. I'm the best mechanic they've got." He winks and takes a sip of his beer.

I shake my head. *And what does she mean, you haven't talked to a ghost yet?*

T chokes and clears his throat after shooting me a glare. *We haven't seen one for me to talk to.*

You saw one the first day you went to the Agency and were too chicken to speak to it.

Yeah, well. It hasn't reappeared. I'm ready for it now, though.

I shake my head. Smythe's gaze bounces between the two of us as if he wants to eavesdrop. Telepathic eavesdropping is his specialty. Or was. Until I learned to build my mental barriers against him.

I'm almost certain I've succeeded. Most of the time, anyway.

"If you are scheduled for work tomorrow, then we can go when you are off," Eloise says.

T's eyes narrow. "Nah, like I said—"

He pauses as I shoot him a 'tell the truth' stare. After a second of silent twin communication, he huffs.

"Fine. I'll go to work tomorrow. I'm off Sunday. Maybe the ghosts will be out then."

"We can try it and see." Eloise smiles at T.

"What'll we do tomorrow?" I face Smythe.

A twinkle sparks in his eyes. One side of his lips turns upward. Uh-huh. I know what he's thinking, and I don't even have to use telepathy.

"I want to know what those minions were doing in the financial counselor's office," he says.

Okay, so that's not what I expected him to say. Since I don't want to broadcast our horizontal activities, I act like his words are no surprise. "You want to know what the minions were up to? Robbing. Killing. General

47

mischief. Pick one."

"What minions?" T glances from me to Smythe and back.

Right. I "forgot" to tell him about our adventures last night.

"We hunted minions to a financial counselor's office last night. Killed them, then Rahab showed up." T's eyes widen, narrowing as my last night's extracurricular activities sink in. I grin at him, unable to keep the smile off my face as I remember the demon's death. "I killed his scaly ass."

T nods, his expression relaxing. "Good. I hate that demon."

"Past tense now. You don't have to worry about him."

"Now that you're done bragging"—Smythe looks at me—"let's discuss how to find out what info those minions tried to steal."

"How do you know they tried to steal info?" For all we knew, they were trying to steal electronics or kill someone in the office. Not that there was anyone else in the office, but still. Killing is a minion specialty.

"Why else would they be in the office?" Smythe's tone makes his question sound more like he's calling me a dumbass.

Which I'm pretty sure he doesn't mean. Anger spikes despite my rationalization. My eyes narrow.

"To kill—"

"Nope." With a single word and shake of his head, he negates my thought. "No one there. And they wouldn't have hidden in the office, even if they knew you were chasing them. It was on the third floor and locked. Besides, hiding isn't in a minion's playbook.

That leaves thievery. We need to determine what they wanted to steal."

"It could've been the electronics. There were some expensive-looking computers in there." Not that I'd recognize an expensive computer if it hit me on the ass, but all the electronics right down to the printers looked much more high-tech than what they had in the hospital. Therefore, more expensive. Right? Right.

"I'll give you that." Smythe nods. "Although I still think they targeted the third-floor office. They could've gone to the local appliance store at the mall down the street and stolen electronics. Why bother with the office? That's why I think they were after information stored on the computers. Not the computers themselves."

He makes more sense than my insistence on the minions breaking in to kill. I hate being wrong. Live and learn, Gin, live and learn.

"Well, when you put it like that." I offer him a half-smile. "I take it I'm doing a little B&E instead of grocery shopping tomorrow?"

Smythe grins. "Now you're talking."

"Well," Eloise says, "Now that we have settled who's doing what, I'll drop back in Sunday morning and pick up T. Maybe we can make contact with the ghost."

T nods. "Hope so."

I raise a brow at him. He glares. I grin. Point made.

"Thank you for dinner, Gin." Eloise smiles my direction. "I should go."

"Would you like to, um, play a game or watch TV or something?" T asks.

Her smile freezes, as if she wants to but isn't sure

she should.

I grab Smythe's hand. "We wanted to go catch a show—"

"We did?"

I give him a not-so-indiscreet kick under the table. "Remember?"

"Oh, yeah. Right. Better go before we're late."

T raises a brow. *Thanks.*

Anytime. Have fun. And don't forget to clean the kitchen.

Say what?

You know. That thing you do where you run water over the dirty dishes and put them in the dishwasher?

Smartass. Get the hell outta here.

My sassy salute leaves him shaking his head.

"Have fun." Eloise waggles her fingers at us.

"Car or portal?" Smythe asks.

"Portal." Traffic in Dallas on a Friday night sucks. A portal might freeze off my exposed parts, but it's better than sitting in congestion on the Central Expressway.

Chapter Six

White walls reflect bright light, disorienting me for a second, until I realize where we are. I stand in the Agency's landing room, the only place to portal into the building. Unless you are Eloise, who possesses the ability to portal anywhere in the building despite wards blocking all entrances except this one. A topic for another day. To my left sits a row of teenage mages, the first line of defense against intruders at the Agency.

Or so I'm told.

Why are we at the Agency? While I didn't one hundred percent believe Smythe was actually going to portal us to a movie, at the same time I never expected him to take us to the Agency.

He knows how much I hate this place.

The overpowering scent of lavender tickles my nose, causing me to scrunch it in defense. Which doesn't work. I sneeze. One of the mages hands me a tissue. I grab the thing with a "thanks," turning to Smythe. "Why are we here?"

His grin holds a sexy promise as he ushers me through the landing room and out into the gilded hallway. "Thought you might want to check out my collection of movies."

"Collection of movies, eh? Is that what you call it nowadays?"

He laughs, the chocolaty tone warm and inviting, a

prelude of things to come. "What would you call it when you stick in a DVD and turn on the TV?"

I waggle my brows as he pushes the elevator button to his third-floor apartment. "Having fun?"

He shrugs. "All right then. Want to go have fun?"

The elevator chooses that moment to arrive, the metallic *ding* interrupting my answer. Not that an answer is needed. He already knows my response.

*****

Bright light wakes me from a deep sleep. A heavy arm lies across my waist. My gaze hops around Smythe's bedroom. While I've been to his apartment several times, I've never slept in his bedroom; he always spent the night at my place. Besides the comfy king-sized bed and two nightstands, his tidy room contains a dresser with a mirror above it.

A painting hangs on the wall next to the bed. I blink several times, finally squinting at the artist's signature. Was that a Monet? A real Monet? Not a print behind glass like I have in my living room, but a real life oil painting that should be hanging in a museum? Holy shit. Smythe was rich.

Or had rich friends who gave awesome gifts.

Or both.

Must be nice. Then again, most of his rich friends lived here at the corrupt Agency, so maybe being poor had its advantages. At least I knew where the money to buy all my house items came from—my job. Or T's. Hard-earned cash.

The Agency, on the other hand, made money hand over fist. Smythe claimed it was from investments or selling off antiquities. After all, the company had been around for millennia.

Except there was way too much pretentiousness for it to be related to those reasons, leading me to believe something else was going on. No wonder Eloise felt a demon in the place. Demons paid well. The question was: what were they paying for?

Less *Justitian* action? Leaving their minions alone? Nope. Wasn't happening on any level in any place in the world. The good guys weren't necessarily winning—being outnumbered tends to make the fight lean toward the demons and minions—but neither were we rolling over exposing our bellies for a death stab.

Maybe I was wrong about demons paying the Agency for who knows what. But I wasn't wrong that the place was corrupt. Someone from the Agency paid Samantha, a blonde bitch mage who hated my guts, to hire minions to kill me. She almost succeeded. David, Smythe's asshat of a father, took her side until we presented enough evidence to convince him otherwise. He still hasn't done anything about her duplicity. Samantha continues to roam the Agency corridors looking for trouble. Or me. Or whatever it is she does when not antagonizing me.

Maybe David's going after the person behind the payments to her account. I'm not holding my breath.

Smythe mumbles, his arm tensing against my waist, snapping me out of my thoughts.

"You awake?"

"Mmmm..." He rolls onto his back, one arm thrown across his eyes. "What time is it?"

I reach for my phone. "Ten."

Yeah, we slept in. Movie night was a lot of fun.

"I don't normally sleep in this late."

I roll to face him. "Feels good, eh? By the way, is

that a Monet?" Pointing a thumb over my shoulder, I gesture to the painting.

"Yeah. It was for sale at auction, so I bought it."

"Must be nice to be able to afford something like that."

He shrugs, rolls off the bed. "Want some coffee?"

"You know that's a rhetorical question." My grin causes him to chuckle.

After a quick stop in the bathroom—thankfully he has a spare toothbrush with my name written on it—I follow the pleasing scent of my morning addiction to the kitchen where the coffeepot perks a happy tune.

"Why, Smythe. I didn't know you drank coffee."

He hands me a supersized mug; the kind addicts use for their morning rush. "I don't."

A wave of happiness washes over me. He bought coffee for me. Along with my size mug. He truly likes me as much as I like him. I wrap my arms around his waist.

"Thank you. You're the best boyfriend a girl could ask for."

He returns the hug, resting his chin on my head. "You're welcome. I hoped..." He swallows. "I hoped you might want to stay here some too?"

"That's why you had a spare toothbrush?"

He kisses me on the cheek and pulls back, his arms still wrapped around my waist. "That and the dentist keeps passing them out like they're candy."

I roll my eyes. "And here I thought you picked it for me."

"Truth hurts."

He smiles. I chuckle, knowing he's teasing. The dentist might have given him one hundred toothbrushes, but he gave one of those to me. More telling, he bought a coffeemaker, coffee, and a supersized mug.

A sure sign of a long-lasting relationship.

I lean my head against his chest. I've fallen head over heels for this man. He's what my heart dreamt of in lonely moments, what my soul longed for in my secret hopes, what I never thought to find. No one, not even Blake, compares to Smythe.

At one time I thought Blake, my former friend with benefits, was the best I could hope for in my screwed-up life. I was devastated when the demon Jezebeth killed him. Or thought I was devastated. Truth be told, Blake's loss didn't strike me as hard as when Smythe thought I'd betrayed him and refused to talk to me. We've moved past the hurt, broken trust and perceived deception. Moved right on past the drama and into a relationship cemented on caring and trust.

I want Smythe for eternity.

But I also want a cup of coffee. To show how happy I am he thought of me. Oh, who am I fooling? I can't live without the stuff.

A kiss later and I pour the black liquid into the pristine white mug and take a sip.

Ah. Bliss. "You chose well."

One shoulder rises and falls in a half-shrug. "It's what you have at your place. But thanks."

He noticed what kind of coffee I drank despite the fact the bag is kept in the fridge and not out on the counter. Now that's saying something. I'm impressed. So I give him another kiss.

At this rate we're never going to leave his apartment.

He pulls away too soon. "We have a busy day and

already overslept. Want me to cook brunch?"

"You know you don't have to ask, right?"

In a move totally uncharacteristic of him, he winks then slaps me on the butt before sauntering to the stove to cook a fabulous brunch.

Gotta love the man.

Chapter Seven

After brunch, we portal to my house for me to shower and change clothes. I might have a toothbrush at Smythe's apartment, but not a spare set of clothes. And there is no way I'm wearing the same outfit two days in a row. Besides, the office we need to break into is in Dallas.

T is at work, pulling one of his once a month Saturday shifts. No sign of Eloise in the house. Did she spend the night? A question for the next time T and I are alone.

I walk into the living room wearing a long-sleeved T-shirt and a pair of blue jeans coupled with running shoes. Not that I use them for their intended purpose. Running and I don't get along. But the shoes are comfy. And as a bonus they're black, suitable for a little B&E at the financial advisor's office.

Smythe sits on the couch, laptop on his thighs in his customary position, fingers dancing across the keys.

"Ready?"

He looks up from the screen, brow furrowed. "For what?"

"I thought we were going to break into the office and see why the minions were there?"

"I am." He points to the laptop, his head tilting to one side. "I didn't mean physically go there."

"Oh. I knew that. Just checking." I should've

known better than to think we were actually portalling into the office. Why portal when Smythe can use his expert hacking skills to obtain entry?

"Uh-huh. Have a seat."

I sit next to him, peering at the screen. As I thought, nothing looks familiar on there. "It's not Windows."

He rolls his eyes. "Watch and learn, Gin, watch and learn."

My lips quirk in a half-grin half-grimace. I do as he says, alternating between looking at the screen and watching his fingers dance across the keys. After awhile, I'm bored and have learned nothing, so I grab the remote and turn the TV channel to HGTV.

Smythe glances up from the laptop, shakes his head, and returns to hacking. Right when the fixed-up house is about to be revealed, he gasps.

"Shit. Didn't see that coming."

Never a good sign. I pry my gaze from the more-expensive-than-I-can-afford interior decorating and look at the laptop. The screen features what looks to be account numbers, but why this is upsetting I have no idea.

"What am I looking at?"

"Account transfers. Not sure if this is what the minions were after, but these are Agency account numbers."

"So? You've said before the Agency gets its money from investments."

"True. But these aren't the investments. It's almost as if someone is paying the Agency."

"How can you tell?" Finance was never my idea of a good time.

"One, this isn't the investment company we use."

"You know what company they use?"

"It's not a secret."

Past conversations click into place. "That's why it took you a while to wonder how the Agency got its money. You knew they invested. I mean, you told me that, but it seemed obvious to me, who knows nothing about finance, that no matter how good the investments, the monetary income was more than what they claimed. Look at all the gold chandeliers in the hallways. Unreal."

"I know. If it's something you've grown up believing, it takes longer to see through the bullshit. They do invest. Just not with this company."

"Maybe they diversified?" Check me out, pulling out the big words.

"These aren't investment accounts." He points at the screen. "These are money transfers. Someone is paying the Agency."

"For what?"

"Good question. Maybe Dad would know."

"You didn't leave on good terms the last time we talked."

"I've talked with him since then."

"He still mad?" Smythe accused his Dad of hiding info. David didn't appreciate being called out. Then again, who likes to be told they're wrong with data to back it up? Pretty much no one.

While his reaction was spot on, the fact he hid info was concerning. Along with him throwing us out of his apartment. The conversation convinced Smythe to see the corruption in the Agency and in his father. Needless to say, Smythe was upset over the matter.

David remains a supersized jerk, but at least Smythe talked things out with him.

"Yeah. He didn't like me accusing him of hiding info."

"Truth always hurts."

"Yeah."

"You guys kiss and make up?"

He rolls his eyes. "No kissing involved. But we're talking."

"You apologize?"

"Hell no. I'm not apologizing for speaking the truth."

I pat his shoulder. "Good for you. Back to the minions. Any clue why they were in the office?"

He focuses on the laptop, eyes narrowed at the screen. "The account is new. First deposit from Little Cub Creek Corporation was yesterday. After the minions broke into the office."

"And you think there's a connection."

He shrugs. "Maybe. Maybe not, but it sure does look suspicious."

"Should we portal to the office and see if we see anything?"

"Eager to break in?"

I shake my head. "Not at all. But I want to know why they were there. Guess I should've asked 'em questions before lopping off their heads."

"Hindsight is everything." A grin twists his lips. "Whatever they left, took, or did, is long gone."

A thought widens my eyes. "What about the security cameras? Maybe they picked up something?"

"The cleanup crew should've erased all evidence of us being there."

"Yeah, I know, but could they recreate what they erased?"

His brows pull in tight, then release as he shakes his head. "Unfortunately, no. Once it's gone, it's gone."

Dammit. "I don't want to add B&E to my list of crimes."

"Then you're in luck. I'll see if I can find more information about this company and why they are giving money to the Agency."

After another house fixer-upper episode, Smythe continues to alternate between tapping keys and tapping his fingers against his leg.

"Mind if I go to the store? I'm out of most of what I eat."

He shrugs. "Sure. This might take a while."

*****

He's still sitting on the couch two hours later when I return. Grocery shopping turned into a longer event than I'd planned. After I put up the groceries, I wrap my arms around his shoulders, giving him a peck on the cheek.

He jumps like he failed to hear me walk up. A quick glance to the corner of his screen and his eyes widen.

"I lost track of time." He places the laptop on the coffee table, stands, and stretches.

"I can see. Whatcha find?"

"There's hardly anything online about the company. I suppose it could be brand new, but there should be much more out there than what I could find. I had better luck hacking into the Agency." He pauses, eyes sparkling as he waits for me to ask.

This should be good.

"Like what?"

"Several companies, all of which have little to no internet footprint, have made donations to the Agency dating back as long as they have digitalized records."

"Wait a minute." I don't want to go here, but it has to be asked. "They made a payment last night, right?"

"Yep." His brow wrinkles.

"And a *Justitian* was killed, right? The Polish *Justitian*?" Cold prickles up my spine as Smythe nods, lips pressed into a thin line. "What if they paid to kill a *Justitian*? What if the companies are demon run and they're paying off the Agency for setting up a *Justitian*?"

A long pause. Smythe's eyes widen.

"They wouldn't do that. Why would the Agency want to kill *Justitians*? We're in the demon killing business, not the *Justitian* killing one."

"But there's a demon at the Agency. Maybe it convinced others to kill off my sword-sisters."

Smythe runs a hand through his hair as he glances to the side. After another long pause, he shakes his head. "I won't totally knock it off the list, but I can't imagine anything like that happening. Even with a demon in the Agency." He sucks in a breath. "Got any other ideas?"

I don't blame him for hopping to a different hypothesis. Thinking of the Agency accepting money from demons to kill *Justitians* gives me the chills. Maybe it's the other way around. Instead of demons paying to kill *Justitians*, companies are paying *Justitians* to kill demons.

At least this idea stops the cold gnawing at my marrow.

"Maybe they're paying off *Justitians* to kill demons? What else would they buy from the Agency?"

"The Agency doesn't sell a *Justitian's* services." A head shake negates my question. "The Agency doesn't sell anything at all. These companies are giving the Agency money, which is then invested in stocks. The payments are a major contributor to the financial wellness of the Agency. Why?"

"Could it be a bribe?"

His brows furrow. "Like protection money?"

"Sure. I guess. I don't know. Outside of balancing a checkbook, finances are not my thing."

"Why would they send the Agency protection money? We don't charge for killing demons and minions."

"Maybe you should?"

He rolls his eyes. "It's for the betterment of the world. We are not mercenaries."

Okay, point taken. While it would be nice if the Agency paid me to kill demons, I do see the point of not being paid for the deed. I'm a nurse, not a mercenary.

But damn, the money to fight demons sure would be nice. A point I'm not going to make at the moment.

"Got it. Then what's your best guess?"

He presses his lips together. Draws in a deep breath and releases it on a sigh. "Let me work on it longer. These things don't happen overnight."

"Should you ask your father?" The last thing I want to do is ask David for anything. Past experience proves he's not likely to help me. But Smythe asks his dad a lot. To no avail. Doesn't stop my mage from continuing to ask, though.

"Not on this. We might be talking again, but…"

A faraway look glazes his eyes.

"I get it. You don't want to screw things up between you. And if you ask and he won't tell you, that'll drive a wedge deeper."

"Yeah. Something like that. I'll keep looking. I have access to the Agency finances and I'll keep digging into the companies paying them. Eventually I'll find something."

Eventually he will. Smythe is nothing if not persistent. Like a one-track-minded dog on the scent of a rabbit, he won't stop until he catches it.

"Are you going to spend the rest of the day hunting?"

He looks at the laptop, then back to me. Another glance at the laptop. He shuts the lid.

"Maybe we can check out a movie?"

Chapter Eight

By the time T comes home from work, Smythe and I have freshened up and have dinner ready.

I give my twin a hug. He smells like sweat and motor oil.

"Let me go change and I'll be right back. It smells good."

As soon as T walks out of the room, I rinse a pot, while talking telepathically to T.

So, how's Eloise? You have fun last night?

I'm not talking about that. He slams our mental connection shut.

Way to go T! I'll take that as a *yes* and will refrain from anything other than a smirk. Maybe. The thought of him and Eloise makes me happy. She's much better than his other girlfriends, although in some ways thinking about the two of them together makes me wonder what they see in each other.

They seem like polar opposites. An auto mechanic and a healer who's been alive for over a hundred years but looks like she's in her mid-thirties. As much as I like Eloise, she's hiding something.

Rather like the Agency who employs her. The difference being Eloise isn't corrupt.

At least, I hope she's not.

T walks back into the kitchen, shoots me a glare, and grabs a beer out of the fridge. I press my lips together. Smythe saves me from breaking my nothing-but-a-smirk promise.

"Are you and Eloise going to the Agency tomorrow?"

T takes a long swallow. "Yep. We're gonna have better luck this time."

Because you're going to admit to seeing a ghost this time? I can't keep the teasing grin off my lips. But so far, I haven't teased him about Eloise. Go me.

He glares. *I only saw it the one time. Then nothing. Give me a break.*

Smythe's gaze hops back and forth between us. He knows we're using our twin telepathic ability to chat, but hopefully can't get through my mental barriers to eavesdrop.

You're fun to tease.

T salutes me with his beer. *Love you too, sis.*

Wanna hand me one of those?

He reaches in the fridge and pulls out a beer. I grab it and pop off the top.

"All that," Smythe waves a hand between T and me, "for a beer?"

"All what?" I take a swallow as my mentor shakes his head.

Pure bliss. A Saturday night with my favorite guys, good food and beer. Life doesn't get much better than this.

*****

By the time I wake Sunday mid-morning, T and Eloise have already left for their find-a-ghost tour of the Agency, leaving me and Smythe to laze around the house. Not that we're lazing. Smythe invited Will over to practice mage magic.

Dr. Will Wunderliech is my long-time friend and fellow co-worker at Blue Forest Emergency Department. Or at least he was until I was placed on leave due to missing too much work fighting demons and minions. My boss Ruth, aka Nurse Hatchet, referred me to a counselor as a condition of getting my nursing job back. Lucky for me, visiting the counselor, Kathy Funk, isn't as horrid as I feared.

Despite having to lie about the reason causing me to visit her office in the first place.

Telling her I was too busy killing demons and minions to report to work would only get me an extended stay in Blue Shores, the hospital's psychiatric ward. No thanks. Been there, done that, managed to live to tell the tale.

When Will arrives, Smythe ushers him to a seat on the living room sofa and proceeds to give a lesson in grounding and centering. Something Will could've used when Perdix, the despair demon, attacked him last week, as Smythe points out.

"I need practice too." Smythe gestures for me to sit on the recliner. "You need practice also."

No complaints from me. Perdix haunted all of us at one time or another, trying to convince us to kill ourselves, to join him in peaceful paradise.

Grounding and centering our thoughts and energy sounds like a great idea.

An hour later, after one failed and one successful attempt to pull energy into my body and pass excess energy into the ground, I leave the two mages to their formation of energy balls. Since I possess no inherent mage magic, forming an energy ball is out of my abilities.

Instead, I clean the kitchen, both bathrooms and my bedroom. Since the men remain on the sofa, ignoring me, I grab my e-reader and relax with a book.

I'm several chapters in when T and Eloise portal into the room. Will extinguishes his energy ball without dropping it on my sofa. Practice makes perfect.

"What did you learn?" Smythe stands, all business and curiosity.

T's eyes glow with excitement. "I talked to the ghost. I know who the demon is."

"It doesn't matter." Eloise shakes her head, her mouth set in a hard line. "He can tell you all he wants, but it makes no sense. He even tried to write it down, but the words blurred."

"Who is it?"

I watch T's lips move, hear his voice, but the words garble in translation between my ears and brain. A headache presses behind my eyes, a splitting pain shattering my concentration. What did my twin say?

I risk opening one eye. When that fails to cause more pain, I peel open the other lid. Smythe rubs his forehead, brows drawn together in pain. Eloise mimics his movements and expression. T looks exasperated, mouth pulled into a frown.

"What's wrong with you guys?" Will glances between all of us, clearly confused.

"Eloise says it's a spell preventing them from knowing who the demon is." T huffs. "I've been trying to tell her, even tried to write it down, but she keeps getting a headache and forgets what I said."

"Demon?" I look at my twin. "Did a ghost tell you who the demon was?"

He rolls his eyes. "I already told you. Told Eloise

three times. I'm not saying his name again."

Him. The demon was a him, not a her. Well, that narrowed it down to about fifty percent of the Agency's employees.

It's a start.

A confused expression remains plastered on Will's face. "If what you say is true about the spell, then how come I could hear you fine with no headache or memory loss?"

"You haven't met the demon." Eloise tugs on T's hand and he guides her to the remaining free chair.

She flops into the seat, still rubbing her forehead.

"You mean the spell only happens if we've met the demon?" Smythe stops rubbing his head and stares at Eloise. "I thought the spell hid their identity."

"As I said earlier, it's a tricky, hard spell." Eloise presses her lips together briefly. "The demon cast the spell over itself. And it appears to only work if you've met the demon."

"Which means we are back to square one, unless we can find a way to eradicate the spell." I look between Eloise and Smythe. "Right?"

"This is ridiculous." T's narrowed eyes and low tone indicate his irritation. "Since neither Will nor I know this demon except by name, maybe we should go hunt him down."

Oh, like that's going to go over well. I straighten, not surprised when Eloise and Smythe mimic my posture.

"No, absolutely not." Smythe glares at T while gesturing to Will. "He's barely learned to form an energy ball and you might be a ghost talker who helped take down a demon, but you can't fight one by yourself.

You'll need help. And I'm not sure if Gin can help you. Clearly she's met this demon since the spell works on her, but her *justitia* only changed once at the Agency and that was shortly before the building was attacked by minions."

"True." I interrupt when he draws in a breath, causing a narrow-eyed glare to fall on me. Too bad. Smythe's glares no longer bother me. "But it has always thought there was a demon at the Agency and acts confused." Especially around David Smythe and Chuck Tweedy. Coincidence or pure luck?

I think David's integrity is lacking, but that doesn't mean he's on the demon's side. Chuck is a complete mystery to me. I don't know the man well enough to judge, although what little I do know is not favorable.

He had no qualms about David using a compulsion spell to try and compel me to spill my secret about Zagan's gift of demonic energy. To be fair, though, the Agency had been attacked by minions and I shot a blast of red demonic power from my sword, which tends to give an Agency boss a case of what-the-fuck.

While I didn't appreciate the attempt at coercion, it didn't mean Chuck was evil.

Nor did it rule it out.

"Do you smell gas?" Eloise sniffs the air, interrupting whatever Smythe was about to say.

Talk of demons and how my *justitia* acts while at the Agency comes to a halt as we all sniff the air.

A slight whiff of gas tingles my nose. I head toward the kitchen. Could I have accidentally flipped on a burner on the stove? The weather wasn't cold enough to turn on the heater, so the only choices were the propane gas grill or my stove. Everyone follows me into the kitchen.

A quick glance at the stove shows all burners turned off. The smell isn't as strong in the kitchen as the living room.

"What about the grill?"

T shakes his head, but heads toward the back door. "We haven't used it since Friday. If the gas was on, we'd have smelled it by now. But I'll check in case."

"Then what—" The rest of my sentence dies as an explosion from the living room rocks my house.

Smythe knocks me to the floor, covering me with his body while screaming a short spell. Good thing it's short. I hit the floor with an '*oomph*', my head slamming into the linoleum, but heat and debris miss us.

I turn my head but can only see the bottom of the cabinets and fridge. Crackles, snaps, and pops echo in my ears. Flames lick the ceiling, smoke fills the kitchen obscuring my view. A pungent burning odor threatens to choke me. Smythe rolls to my side, a wrinkle drawing his brows together.

Thank god for his spell. Without it, I'd be—

My thought stutters to a stop as my brain focuses on who else is in the room. Oh god, T? Did the spell protect my twin? Will? Eloise?

T!

Here! There's some sort of cushion around me. I can't move but I'm not hurt. You?

Smythe cast a spell. Do you see—

"I'm going to try to portal us out of here." Smythe interrupts my conversation. I can barely hear his voice above the roar of the fire.

"Where's everyone else?"

Karilyn Bentley

"Hopefully my spell worked on them. Be quiet."

Sweat beads on his forehead as he turns his palm toward the ceiling. A couple of words into the portal spell and my *justitia* shifts into a sword.

What the hell?

I shift my gaze from Smythe toward what used to be the living room. A fireman dressed in full gear including a mask walks through the wall of flame. I can't see his lips but I'm pretty sure they are turned into a shit-eating grin. Since it's highly doubtful the fire department made it to my house in under a minute and my *justitia* is no longer a bracelet, I'm also pretty sure this is a minion in a fireman disguise.

"Fuck!" Smythe grabs my arm as I start to rise, keeping me against the floor. "Don't get up! You'll break the spell!"

I second his choice of curse words. The minion takes a step closer. I point my sword at him while lying on my back. Unless he decides to impale himself on it, I'm not much of a threat.

Gin! T breaks through my concentration. *Eloise got me out! We're in the backyard.*

Smythe! Using our telepathic connect, I shout into Smythe's mind. He stops muttering his portal-forming words and glances at me.

I give him a quick glance before focusing on the slowly approaching minion. *T and Eloise are out. You only need to get Will and me through the portal.*

Smythe nods, resuming his spell, while I study the minion's movements. The damn thing stops moving when he gets within a foot of my feet. Yep, he definitely wears a shit-eating grin. He reaches an arm over his shoulder as if trying to grab a sword. The air

72

shimmers for a second before the icy cold of a portal surrounds me.

We land on grass, Will a couple of feet from us. T rushes to my side, hand outstretched as if to help me up until he notices the sword jutting across the back of my hand. Smythe rolls to his feet. I grab T's retreating hand with my left palm and haul myself upright. Eloise stands behind us, eyes closed as she faces the burning house.

Oh god. My home is burning. All of my things, destroyed.

Everything I've worked for incinerated in billowing smoke and red-orange fire.

The *justitia* shimmies a little dance against my wrist. *Minion! Kill the minion!*

I jump, dropping T's hand. He runs both hands over his head, eyes wide, cheeks pale.

"We need to kill that minion." Smythe gestures toward the house.

He's got to be kidding. Without his spell protecting me, I'll die. "How the hell am I supposed to do that? My home is burning down!"

As if in answer to my question, the fireman-imitating minion bursts through the backdoor onto the porch. Sirens sounds in the distance, wailing screams drawing closer. I pay them little attention, my full focus on the damn minion who destroyed my house.

He pulls off his mask, dropping it onto the ground, his lips pulled into a you're-dead smile.

"Son of a bitch." T murmurs.

Agreed. That minion walking toward us is going down.

My scream joins the wailing sirens as I run toward

the destroyer of my home. The minion pulls a sword from a back sheath. Of course he does. I swear there's a Swords-R-Us for demonic entities. I draw my arm back, ready for a killing blow, the minion mirroring my movements. Right before we engage, an energy ball slams into the minion's chest, knocking him back a step.

Unfortunately, the minion remains upright, a puzzled expression on his face as he swipes at where the energy ball smacked into his chest. Both the minion and I turn to the side, staring at Will who stands with smoking fingers. He waves his hands in the air as if they're on fire. Which they can't be since I've seen Smythe throw energy balls and his fingers never smoke.

Maybe it's because Will's a newbie mage?

"Watch out!" Smythe yells.

My arm moves of its own volition, courtesy of the *justitia*, who grabs control of my movements.

Good thing too. The minion recovered while I stand staring as the smoke dissipates from Will's fingers. Without the entity taking control, I would have been injured.

How dare this minion set fire to my home and try to kill me. A bolt of rage burns through my system, consuming me with its searing heat even as it fuels my swing.

Thanks to the *justitia* taking control, I move so fast everything around me blurs. The minion doesn't stand a chance. One swing and his head rolls on the dry grass. Blood spatters my clothes, pooling on the ground beneath the no-longer-walking evil.

Using the flat of the sword, I catch the gray mist escaping the minion's body. On a normal day, the mist sizzles as it touches the *justitia*, but the crackle from my burning house dampens the sound. Whatever demon sent this minion just got a little weaker thanks to the power of the *justitia*. Kill enough of its minions and the demon dies.

As the *justitia* morphs into a bracelet, I draw in a deep breath. And cough as smoke and the stench of my burning house fills my lungs.

"Gin! Get the hell away from the house!" Smythe yells from where everyone stands pressed against the fence as far away from the flames as they can get and still be in my yard.

I glance over my shoulder at the house. During my fight, the fire spread into an inferno of red-orange death. A wall of heat presses toward me, a roar of danger. Small tendrils jump onto my neighbor's house, wisps of smoke rising from their roof.

My home. My life. All my belongings. Destroyed.

An overwhelming urge to drop and cry competes with the need to run to the others. T screams in my head, but I'm frozen, rooted to the ground, watching all I worked for go up in smoke.

Someone grabs my arm, shakes me hard, yanks me away from the flames. I stumble, loose my balance, but Smythe hauls me to my feet. His lips move as if he's talking but the only sound I hear is the roar of the flame, the crackle of wood, the destruction of me.

I keep looking back, watching my house burn, as Smythe pulls me forward until we stand with the others. Heat bombards us here too. T grabs me, pulls me into a hug.

"I thought the flames were going to get you."

"I wasn't that close."

"Yeah, you were." Will steps closer.

I glance between my twin, Will, and Smythe. "Where's Eloise?"

"She took the minion away." Smythe runs a clinical glance down the front of my body. "I'm not the best at this spell, but I should be able to remove enough of the blood so the first responders don't notice." He waves a hand over my blood-spattered clothes, rinsing away the stain with a spell.

Normally I'd be impressed. Instead, all I manage is a thanks.

Sirens screech to a stop in front of my home, red and blue lights flashing across the neighboring houses. Real firemen, not minions imitating firemen, rush around the corner of my home, tearing through the side gate as if it doesn't exist. After spotting us, one of the men rushes toward us, the others head to the house.

"What happened?"

"We heard an explosion." Smythe answers for me. "We were in the kitchen and the explosion came from the living room." He points in that direction. "We managed to get out but weren't able to grab anything."

"We need to get you away from here. This whole yard isn't safe." He glances around as if looking for a gate away from the house. His clothes might protect him from the flames, but ours could easily catch on fire.

"We'll jump the fence."

Good thing the fence is chain-link and only four feet tall. Hopping it is a breeze. We cross into the neighbor's yard, then out onto the street. The crowded street.

Saturday night entertainment in the neighborhood: watching Gin's house burn.

Held back by a sense of self-preservation, my neighbors flood onto the sidewalk opposite my house, pointing at the fire trucks, shaking their heads at the flames leaping toward the night sky. A few give worried glances from my house to theirs, clearly nervous about a spark landing on their roof. The firemen hustle around their truck, dragging a hose to the conveniently located fire hydrant, and pointing the other end at my house.

But not even the heavy stream of water douses the flames. Another explosion sends a blast of fire ripping outward, like a great beast searching for an easy kill. The fireman holding the hose stumbles back, ducking his head against the blast of heat. Neighbors gasp, shuffle off the sidewalk.

"Dayum." One of the neighbor's shakes his head. "I hope that don't spread to my house."

And that's when I start crying.

Chapter Nine

Smythe holds me as I sob on his shoulder. T pats my back. I don't need to hop inside my twin's head to know he's as upset as I am even if he's not crying like a baby. He lived there too. I'm not the only one who lost everything.

I pull away from my mentor's arms, wiping my face with my hands. When that fails to work, I use the back of my shirt sleeve. Not too ladylike but the long-sleeved shirt wipes my face dry. I draw in a ragged breath.

Will pats my shoulder. "I'm sorry, Gin."

I sniff. Offer him a small nod.

A female cop walks over to us, stopping in front of a group of neighbors. "Do you know who owns the house?"

The neighbors shake their heads, while I step forward. "I do."

A little buzz of excitement ignites a low murmuring that spreads through the crowd. Nothing like gossip to liven things up.

The cop walks to where we stand. "You own the house?" No need to explain which house.

"I do. My brother lives with me." I tilt my head toward T, who steps to my side.

"I'm sorry about your home."

I nod, shock rendering me short on words. And

judging from the tear and snot dampened shirt sleeve, short on niceties too.

"I'm Officer LaShanda Johnson." She flashes her badge then pulls out a notepad and pen. "Can you tell me what happened?"

I take a deep breath, but once again, Smythe saves me from speaking.

"We were in the living room and smelled gas. We all went into the kitchen to see where it was coming from and that's when the explosion happened. We barely made it out of the house."

The fireman-imitating minion who later tried to lop off my head with his sword, forcing me to return the favor, was wisely left out of the narrative.

"Who are you?" Her pen hovers over her notepad as her gaze narrows on Smythe.

"Aidan Smythe. Gin's boyfriend."

"Right." Her attention snags on me. "Give me your full name."

"Gin Crawford. G-I-N."

Officer Johnson raises a brow but makes no comment on my name. After noting my name, she turns to T. "And your name is—"

"T Crawford."

"That short for something?"

T scowls. "Yeah. Tonic."

Officer Johnson blinks, her lips pressing together as she struggles not to grin. "Gin and Tonic?"

I shrug. "Our parents stuck with a theme."

"Mmm. And your name?"

"Dr. Will Wunderliech."

This time she loses the battle with the grin. But only for a second and then she's all business. "Okay.

Ms. Crawford. Is there a number where you can be reached?"

I give her my cell number, my voice trailing off at the last number. "But my phone is in my house."

"I'm sorry."

"You can call me until Gin gets another phone." Smythe gives the cop his number.

"Do you have a place to stay?"

When I pause, Smythe answers for me. "She'll stay with me."

Thank you.

He nods at my telepathic appreciation.

Officer Johnson shoots me an 'are you okay with that' look. I nod and offer her a smile.

She snaps her notepad closed. "Again, I'm sorry for your loss. If you think of anything else, give me a call."

"Will do." Right. Like I'm going to tell her about the minion. Or Eloise's disappearing act with the thing.

Officer Johnson sticks her pen and pad in her front pocket and faces the neighbors. She raises both of her hands.

"Okay, folks, enough staring. Move along so the firemen can work."

My neighbors follow her directions, moving to the edge of the perimeter she establishes to give the firemen room to work. An ambulance arrives as we are moving to where she gestures. Of course they want to check out the four of us, surprise etching their faces when they realize we don't suffer from smoke inhalation or burns.

Hopefully that won't lead the detectives to assume we blew up my home.

Hours later, after the fire department saves the houses on either side of mine and puts out the fire that burned my home to black charred wooden beams, the stench of burned wood fills the autumn air. I sit on the curb, staring at the remains of my home as firemen stomp through it, confirming the lack of fire.

Most of the neighbors have wandered back to their houses, the few left stand in small circles. Despite living here for seven years, I don't know my neighbors well. Several offer me condolences, their names and offers of help drifting past my muddled mind.

A faint ringing snaps my attention from the destruction to Smythe, who pulls his phone from his pocket, swipes across the screen and puts it against his ear.

"Yeah? Still here... Uh-huh... You'll have to come. Unless you want them going through the landing room?"

Those last words make me think he's talking to Eloise. I lean closer. Easy to do since he sits next to me.

"Yeah, that's what I thought... No, not now. Too many people. I'll call when it's safe."

He ends the call and places the phone into his pocket. I raise a brow, silent speak for was that Eloise and what did she want. A grin turns his lips. T and Will glance at him.

But before he can speak, one of the firemen walks toward us. I stand.

"Ms. Crawford. We've finished putting out the fire, but you won't be able to cross the yellow line for at least twenty-four hours. I'm sorry for your loss."

"Thank you for your help."

He nods before walking back to the rest of his

team. Once the man is safely across the street helping to ready for departure, Smythe speaks.

"Eloise called."

Ah-ha. I knew it. Usually I'd make a smartass remark or grin or something to let him know I guessed right. Tonight, though, I'm exhausted, a bone tiredness rendering me unable to form a gotcha response. Instead of saying anything, I blink. Blinking uses a hell of a lot less energy.

"Once everyone else leaves, she'll portal in and we'll take you back to the Agency for the night."

"Or y'all can come to my place." Will offers. "I have enough beds for everyone. And it's closer."

I glance at T.

I'd rather stay at the Agency.

Me too.

"Thanks, Will." I give his arm a squeeze. "But we need to talk to Eloise"—about where she disposed of the minion, among other things—"so we'll go tonight with Smythe. Maybe later? I'll definitely need someplace to stay for awhile."

"Sure. Whatever. Just wanted to throw it out there. I have a big house. You both need a place to stay." He shrugs.

I wrap my arms around him. "You're a good friend, Will. Thank you."

Was he blushing?

Smythe clears his throat. "You can come too, Will."

"Nah. Unless you really need me to?"

Smythe shakes his head.

"Then I'll go on home. Can't leave until they move their trucks. They're blocking me in."

I glance to the fire trucks. Yep, definitely blocking in Will's car. But not for long. The firemen load their equipment into the trucks, climb aboard, and drive off into the night, the cop car and paramedics following them. As if given permission to move, the remaining neighbors shuffle off to their houses.

After a few minutes, Will, Smythe, T and I are the only ones left standing on the sidewalk.

"You sure you don't want to come over?" Will glances between T and me.

Both of us nod but I answer. "Thanks again but we're covered for tonight."

"You know how to reach me."

He gives me a hug before leaving. Smythe wastes no time calling Eloise while walking into the shadows between two houses. As Will drives off, Smythe walks back to us holding Eloise's arm.

T elbows me in the side, his voice a low whisper. "Why did Eloise portal back? Why not just meet her there?"

"I don't think Smythe wants the landing room to record your presence."

He nods as Smythe and Eloise meet us.

"I'm sorry about your home, Gin. And T." Eloise places a hand on my shoulder. "I wish I could repair it for you and return all your lost items."

"Thank you, Eloise." I give her a hug.

As soon as I release her, T wraps his arms around her, sans words.

"Why don't you want us going through the landing room?" I ask Smythe.

"I don't want anyone to know you two are at the Agency."

"Why? Not that I'm complaining about not having to land in the white room. That place always makes me sneeze."

A grin flickers across his lips, an internal struggle not to laugh. "Sneeze, huh?" His expression grows serious. "In all truthfulness, I don't know why. Instinct. Eloise has the same feeling."

An idea pops into my brain. "You both think the minion who set my house on fire has something to do with the demon at the Agency."

He shrugs. "It could. Better safe than sorry."

"I can believe it." T keeps an arm around Eloise's shoulders as he turns to face us. "After learning who the demon is, it doesn't surprise me."

"You know who the demon is?" Surprise laces Eloise's voice.

T rolls his eyes, gives a little huff. "Yeah. For like the twentieth time, it's—"

Whatever he says next is lost in a sudden, pounding headache. I rub a hand across my forehead trying to alleviate the pulsing behind my eyes. I swear someone exploded a mini-bomb in my head. Come to think of it, I've been getting a lot of headaches lately. There's a reason.

If I could only remember what the reason was. I don't have a tumor, do I? A shot of panic ricochets through my system at the thought. But a quick glance proves Eloise and Smythe also have a headache, judging from the way they rub their heads. Whew. It's not a tumor. Unless we all contracted one at the same time. And the chances of that happening are pretty much nonexistent. Circling back to the original question: why do we all have headaches?

Which takes us to important question number two: what were we talking about before a headache derailed the conversation?

"Geesh." T shakes his head. "That spell gets you every time. We get further if I don't mention the name of the Agency demon."

That's right. A spell. A couple of days ago, Eloise mentioned a spell caused our headaches. A spell cast by a powerful demon to conceal their identity.

Damn powerful spell to make us forget their name and our discussion about them. We need a counterspell STAT. Headaches and memory loss aren't productive toward solving the identity of the Agency demon.

Which is obviously why the creature cast the spell in the first place.

Damn demons.

"You know who the Agency demon is?" Excitement laces Smythe's voice.

T rolls his eyes to Heaven as if asking for assistance at my mentor's question. His reaction tells me we've been over this before.

"As I keep saying. Yes, I know who it is. But you can't understand me. The spell prohibiting you from knowing? Remember that one?"

Smythe rubs the bridge of his nose. "I do. How many times have you told us their identity?"

"A hundred? Shit, man, I don't know the number. Does it matter? What we need to do is figure out a way for you to know without the spell taking effect."

"And we're not going to do that out here in the middle of the street. Come on, we'll go back to the Agency. My room isn't bugged so we can talk in there."

Smythe leads us to the same shadows where Eloise

appeared in a portal. We clasp hands as Eloise speaks the portal-forming words. My gaze focuses on the ruined, charred shell of what used to be my house. The symbol of me making it in life. My home. Destroyed. Nothing but black beams and charcoaled scraps remaining.

A lump blocks my throat as the portal swallows me into its icy depths. Gone. My life is gone. Exploded in a rush of flame and evil. A flash of anger drives away the tears, burns them into a cold vapor of steel resolve. Whoever set my house on fire is going down. They destroyed what was mine. I'll destroy what is theirs.

Vengeance is mine, thus sayeth the *Justitian*.

The portal spits us out into Smythe's apartment at the Agency. Tingles spread across my skin when I exit the portal as if I crossed an electric wire. Not only am I shivering, which is a normal portalling experience for me, but now a feeling of small electrical shocks run up and down my limbs.

The help-I've-been-electrocuted feeling subsides as soon as both feet touch the carpet in the apartment. Smythe and T shake their arms for a second after landing. Eloise steps free of the portal like the shocked experience was nothing new. Clearly it wasn't for her.

"What the hell was that?" I shake my hands and the tingling disappears.

"Wards." Eloise heads toward the sofa, familiar enough with the layout of the apartment to not need help navigating. "If you bypass the landing room, you have to pass through the wards and they tingle a bit."

"How can you create a passage through the wards?" Smythe furrows his brows as he stares at her. "No one is supposed to enter this building without going through the landing room."

"We've been through this before, Aidan." Her voice holds a warning. Not that my mage pays it any attention.

"Yeah, and you still haven't told me how you manage it. Why can't you explain the spell to me?"

"It wouldn't work."

A long pause as he waits for her to say why not. She doesn't. Smythe's forehead wrinkle grows deeper.

"Again. Why. Not?"

Another long pause. This time emotions flit across Eloise's face too fast for me to catch. When she speaks, her voice is quiet, timid. A tad embarrassed. And yet an undercurrent of irritation threads through her words.

"They don't ward the building to keep out my kind."

Red tinges Smythe's cheeks. "I didn't realize. I thought it was a spell. Forget I asked."

T glances between them. "Didn't realize what? What do you mean 'your' kind?"

What did she mean? Clearly she's not referring to her cougar status with my brother.

"It's okay," Smythe hurries his words. "You don't have to—"

"Trust flows both ways, Aidan." Eloise takes a deep breath. "The building is only warded against demons and humans. The wards focus portalling humans into the landing room while blocking demons from entering. If you travel with me, then you can portal wherever I go because my portal cancels the warding effect on humans. The wards don't exist for my kind. I'm nephilim."

T blinks. "Come again?"

"Nephilim." Her lips form a hard line. "Half angel, half human."

I blink, remembering Perdix, the despair demon, claiming he couldn't touch me because I was too well protected by an 'other.' My *justitia* called the 'other' an abomination. Smythe remained mute on the matter. Now I know why. He didn't want to give away Eloise's secret.

Although I don't understand why my *justitia* considers a half angel-half human an abomination. Or why Eloise seems a mixture of embarrassed and angry.

"You're an angel?" If T's eyes got any bigger they'd take over his face.

"Half angel. There's a difference."

"Whatever. That's cool."

Eloise's head snaps up. "You think it's cool?"

He shrugs. "Sure. I mean, look at all the stuff you can do. You wouldn't be able to do any of it if you were a regular human healer, now would you?"

"I guess not."

"I've told you before," Smythe says, "your ancestry doesn't matter."

"Maybe not to you but it's highly offensive to the angel half of my family." Her lips press together. "That's how I ended up living with the demons. After Mother died, I was kicked out and thought to get back at them by turning to their mortal enemies for aide." She shakes her head. "Big mistake. That's why the Agency didn't trust me when I came to them offering my healing services. They knew I'd lived with demons. Although I managed to convince them it was not by my choice."

"I didn't realize your whole story." Smythe appears

nonplussed.

T blinks.

I skip her background—having a bad one myself I understand the need not to bring up memories best left forgotten—and focus on the present.

"Are you protecting me?"

She turns to me, one brow raised. "I'm sorry?"

"Topic change much, Gin?" Smythe mirrors her expression.

"Sorry. I'm sorry you had an awful childhood but glad you made it to the Agency because I wouldn't be here without you. But what I really want to know is if you're the one Perdix said was my protector?"

"A demon said that to you?" Her head tilts a little to the side.

"Yep." I glance at my red-cheeked lover. He knew who my protector was and refused to tell me. I want confirmation from Eloise.

She sighs. "All my secrets out in the open. Yes, I protect you. Or try to. I can't always be there, but I come when you're hurt. You are the last of your line and I made a promise to your great-grandmother. I have not always been successful with protecting your family, but I'm trying. How did the demon know?"

"No clue and he's no longer alive to ask. Did you cast a spell on me he could see?"

"No." She shakes her head. "I simply try to be around when you need me. No spell. Besides the healing ones and you know about those."

"Interesting. And thank you for the protection. And the multiple healings." Especially the healings. I'd be dead if it wasn't for Eloise coming to my aide.

"Despite my best intentions, the healing is all the

protection I've been able to give."

I fidget during the long pause after she speaks. How did Perdix know Eloise protected me? Did other demons realize the same thing? Why was a nephilim considered an abomination?

A question for Smythe. No way was I asking Eloise about her abomination status. Clearly she'd been raised to believe she was below worthless. And yet managed to rise above it. Rather like my experience. Not the exact same thing, but the emotional impact was similar. I knew better than to ask her. I'd follow up with Smythe after Eloise left.

"Now that we have that out in the open." Smythe clears his throat. "Let's discuss the demon here."

T rolls his eyes toward the ceiling. An expression he's been doing a lot lately. "This is an exercise in futility. You got any beer?"

"No I don't and no it's not. At least not for us. We need a game plan."

"We had a game plan," I point out. "T was supposed to talk to the ghost and tell us who the demon was. He did. We can't remember what he told us. We need to break the spell."

"Any ideas on how to break it, Eloise?"

She sucks in half her lip, clicking her tongue, deep in thought. "You'd need a demon to break the spell. It's more complicated than I can perform."

"How are we supposed to do that? We're not going to call up a demon to chat. We need another way."

I raise my hand, gaining me an odd look from Smythe.

"What, Gin? This isn't a classroom."

"Yeah, well." I offer him a grin. He shakes his

head, his eyes twinkling as I speak. "I have an idea. Why don't we ask Zagan?"

Chapter Ten

Smythe stares at me, eyes wide, the previous twinkle disappearing at the onset of surprise. Heat floods my cheeks as he continues to stare, waiting for me to retract my words. Not happening.

I clear my throat. "What? It's a valid option."

"No. Just no." He shakes his head. "You are not under any circumstances contacting Zagan. It's bad enough he talks to you without you calling him."

"He talks to you?" Surprise laces Eloise's voice.

"He marked her." Smythe interjects. "I thought you knew that."

Eloise sucks in a breath. "No. I did not."

"He tried to make me his servant by giving me a mark on my neck. It didn't work."

Relief weaves through her features. A shame that same relief hadn't travelled to my twin. T resembles an irate man sucking on a persimmon. Good to know nothing changed in his I-hate-demons-talking-or-fighting-with-my-sister attitude. I give him a short head shake, a nonverbal drop-it.

Smythe makes a little motion with his hand. Looks like Eloise isn't the only one spilling secrets tonight.

"My *justitia* thinks of Zagan as a friend."

Relief morphs to shock as Eloise gasps. I rush my next words.

"They know each other from the beginning. Zagan

created the bracelets. The entity in mine was his servant, his friend. Some of that friendship leaks into me." I refuse to state Zagan knew me long before I wore the bracelet, long before I became a *Justitian*. No need to spill how he gave me strength to lie for years. Some secrets should remain untold. "I think he'd come if I asked."

Problem was: I didn't know how to ask, having never had a desire to call up the demon for a chat. He always came to me. Unasked.

Smythe negates my observation with a quick head shake. "I don't care. We'll find another way."

"I agree." Eloise says. "We'll search the library tomorrow. Hopefully there will be a counterspell."

I'm not so hopeful. No, make that I'm a realist. The Agency library might have a ton of scrolls, but I doubt a single one contains the counterspell. Smythe's research would've turned it up by now.

Provided he knew to look.

Did he already look for it? I feel like the Agency demon's spell has turned my mind into Swiss cheese.

"I'm down with anything where you don't have to talk to a demon." T crosses his arms. "It's bad enough a minion set our house on fire. Who do you think he was working for?"

I rub the bridge of my nose. Until T spoke, I'd managed to compartmentalize the loss of my home into a small area of my mind. Covered it up with talk of Eloise's past and the Agency demon. Left it alone until I needed to deal with the ramifications.

But with the mention of my destroyed house, the lock on the compartment breaks free, sending emotions pinging through my veins. Soul deep pain renders my limbs a trembling mess. I cover my face with my hands, trying to draw in a deep breath instead of the shallow gasps bringing little oxygen into my lungs.

Get a grip, Gin. Get a grip. Self-talk refuses to help.

Smythe gathers me into his arms, stroking a hand up and down my back as I sob. I am definitely not getting a grip.

Then again, I lost everything. I deserve a little crying.

Unfortunately, what I'm doing cannot be considered a little crying. More like a tsunami of tears.

And through it all Smythe holds me, lends me his strength, until I sniff the last sob into oblivion. Good thing he doesn't mind his shirt being wet.

When Smythe releases me after who knows how long, T steps into my line of vision. He touches my shoulder, his grief flowing through me. I'm not the only one who lost everything tonight. It was his home too. His sense of belonging. Not as strong as mine—I bought the house after all—but still present in the undertones of his grief.

"We'll be okay, sis. We'll get through this." *Just like we always have.*

I nod, my head still on Smythe's shoulder. The meaning behind his words reminds me I need to tell him Smythe knows our secret. Not a conversation I'm looking forward to. And not a conversation I'll be starting tonight.

One problem at a time.

Although I should tell him something's up.

T, when this mess is over, there's something we need to discuss.

His brow furrows. *Okay. Just not now.*

I release Smythe and hug my twin. "Yeah." I sniff. "We'll be fine. Eventually."

"T has a point." Smythe pats my back. "Why did the minion target you?"

"Don't they do that? I mean, they always seem to know I'm a *Justitian*. There are only thirteen of us in the world, so it would be logical to assume demons and their minions know who we all are. Maybe one of them decided one less *Justitian* in the world would be a good thing."

Smythe cocks his head to the side, gives a half-shrug. "I guess. It's happened before but not often. Demonic entities usually prefer fighting a *Justitian* instead of a subterfuge attack. It's an unspoken agreement between us, fighting rather than assassination." The corners of his eyes tense and release a couple of times. "Although we did invade Zagan's home with intent to kill. Maybe it's payback."

"First off, we didn't kill Zagan." Although I had gone along with the demon's plan to make it look like I killed him. The big reason Smythe didn't trust me for a long while. "Second, that would imply Zagan sent the minion. He wouldn't kill me." Make me his servant, sure. Give me power to kill his enemies so he could take over Hell, definitely. Kill me? Nope, no way.

Smythe tilts his head to the side. "Point taken. But I still say the minion tonight targeted you."

"I'm not saying he didn't. If they knew who I was and wanted to get rid of a *Justitian*, then they targeted me."

"I meant more along the lines of they wanted *you* specifically gone. Not you as a *Justitian* but you as Gin

Crawford."

I blink a couple of times as the thought settles into a pulse racing, breath stealing experience. "You mean a demon wanted me specifically dead? Like they had a personal grudge against me, Gin, not me the *Justitian*?"

"Yep." He nods.

"Well, doesn't that put a cherry on the whipped cream of my very bad fucked up sundae."

A demon or minion putting me in their proverbial crosshairs was par for the job. Nothing personal about it. But a demonic entity coming after me because I'm Gin Crawford made my stomach roll and threaten to evacuate its contents.

If not to kill me for being a *Justitian*, why would a demon want me?

"Goddamn it, Gin. Can't you take that bracelet off?" T crosses his arms and glares at my wristwear as if the expression will scare the thing into hopping off my arm.

I shoot him a go to hell glare. He knows the answer to his rhetorical question.

Smythe ignores my twin. "If only there was a way to tell which demon the minion who blew up your house serves. Then we could track that demon."

"And what?" I raise a brow. "Hope they spill why they want me dead?" Smythe shrugs. I roll my eyes. "Come on. Besides, you don't have a spell to tell how a minion belongs to a demon without seeing the two together. Speaking of, why not? After a millennium hunting these things, wouldn't some mage at the Agency have figured out a spell for determining a minion's demon?"

Fire flashes in Smythe's eyes. He opens his mouth.

But Eloise is the one who speaks. "It wasn't a mage. But there is a spell for identification."

Chapter Eleven

Morning sun brushes a finger of light across my cheek, waking me from a pleasant dream. The dream evaporates as soon as I open my eyes.

I lie on my side in Smythe's bed, one of his heavy arms thrown across my waist. The scent of sex lingers on the sheets and invades my senses. I sigh and grin.

After Eloise told us the spell to determine a minion's demon, she and T beat a retreat to her apartment, located three floors above Smythe's. Smythe and I went to bed, but not immediately to sleep.

And now morning sun greets me. Happy Monday.

Oh shit. It's Monday. I'm supposed to be at my counselor's at nine. A quick peek at the clock shows it's twenty till nine. Uh oh! If I want to keep my job, I need to get to Kathy Funk's office.

Or call and move my appointment. After all, my house burned down last night and I'm pretty sure a detective will be calling me about it today. Not to mention, Smythe and I plan on performing the demon finding spell this morning. No time for a counselor.

I sniff at the thought of my demolished home. I want to pull the covers over my head and cry for an eternity, but I have too much to do. And crying might make me feel better, but it wouldn't accomplish anything on my to-do list.

Lifting Smythe's arm, I roll out of the bed, grab my

clothes off the floor and Smythe's phone off the nightstand, and dash to the bathroom. After bathroom duties and a quick swipe with the toothbrush, I call Kathy's office.

"Funk Counseling," the receptionist answers the phone. "How may I help you?"

"This is Gin Crawford, I have an appointment at nine? I need to move it to later this week. My house burned down last night."

"Oh my goodness. I'm so sorry to hear that. We can see you at nine in the morning on Thursday?"

"Sounds good. Thanks."

"I'm so sorry about your house."

"Yeah. Me too. See you Thursday."

I end the call.

"Who was that?"

At Smythe's question, I jump at least a foot in the air. He stands right behind me. Damn sneaky mage. Luckily, I managed to hold on to the phone.

I turn to face him. "Geez Louise. Scare a girl, why don't you?"

"I thought you heard me." He wraps me in his arms.

I pull back, giving him my best smile. "That was my counselor. I changed this morning's appointment to Thursday afternoon. Figured I could do so since my house burned down."

I ignore the stab of sorrow at the thought.

He gives me a peck on the cheek. "Okay. When did you want to go to your house and try out that spell?"

"After breakfast?"

"Sounds good."

****

After breakfast and three large mugs of coffee, we portal to the shadows of my neighbor's house. The scent of burned wood hangs heavy in the November air. I step into the warm sunlight, my house directly across the street, its charcoaled shell a blot on the middle-class neighborhood.

I swallow.

Yellow tape outlines the perimeter of the yard, a warning not to explore the burned-out house. A strange silence permeates the neighborhood, as if the other houses on the block mourn the loss of mine.

Smythe pauses for a moment before giving my hand a squeeze. "Come on. Let's get this done before someone drives by."

"Shouldn't the fire investigator be here?"

He shrugs, looking both ways before crossing the street, his hand clasped firmly around mine. Clearly, what happens after a fire was put out is not on his list of knowledge.

The sight of my house strikes like a sucker punch to the stomach. I can't draw in a deep breath. Although that could be because of the strong stench of fire coating the air.

Smythe leads me around to the backyard, to where I killed the minion. With a simple thought, the minion sensors in my eyes activate. Dark red-orange trails dart from the back door to a spot in the yard still dotted with dried blood.

I point at the blood pool. "Might want to clean that before anyone notices."

"Shit. I should've called the cleanup crew last night but got distracted."

"At least Eloise vanished the minion." Although I

forgot to ask her where she put the thing.

The sentence is barely finished before his phone is against his ear. "Yeah, need a cleanup crew to Gin's. The place burned down last night due to a minion catching it on fire and there's a blood stain in the grass needing to be erased." He nods, ending the call.

"They'll be here in a minute." He places a warm hand on my shoulder. "Hopefully the inspector or cops or whoever comes after a fire haven't come yet."

"Yeah. I forgot about the blood last night. Was a little busy."

"As well you should be. Not only were you fighting a minion, but your house burned down as you watched."

My words die on my lips as a portal forms. The same crew who cleaned the financial advisor's office steps into the yard. The lead mage shakes her head as she looks at the house.

"Man, that's horrid." Her gaze turns to me. "Sorry about your loss."

"Thanks. Me too."

After Smythe points out the pool of dried blood and emphasizes the need for speed, he leaves the cleanup crew to magically scrub the yard of minion bits.

"Come on, Gin. Let's give them room to work." He leads me to the side of the house where the fire started, pausing by the chain-link fence.

"Aren't we going to do the spell?"

Giving the cleanup crew a narrow-eyed glance, he shakes his head. "What if they're spies for the Agency demon?"

Damn. I should've thought of that one. I glance to

the mages. "Good point."

A shudder grips my limbs. Who could we trust?

We lean against the fence, watching as the cleanup crew erases evidence of the minion. Since there isn't much to clean, they are finished a couple of minutes later. But all the evidence is gone. Since they did their job correctly, does that mean they can be trusted?

Dammit. I hate not knowing.

"Is that all?" The female mage approaches us.

Smythe nods. "Thank you."

"Anytime." She walks back to the others, forms a portal, and they disappear inside.

As soon as we are alone, Smythe pulls out a piece of paper containing the words to the spell. He reads through it a couple of times, lips mouthing the words. I watch him in rapt silence. Part of me is surprised he needs to learn a spell. For some inane reason, I believed he knew all the spells. And if he didn't, all he needed to do was glance at a scroll in the Agency library and poof, spell memorized.

It strikes me as odd he needs to learn spells like everyone else.

The other part of me finds it comforting to realize he lacks a photographic memory.

Yep, I'm hopping down the rabbit trail of weirdness.

"Stand over here." Smythe's words snap me out of my thoughts.

I move to where he gestures. He holds the spell in front of him as he speaks in a strange language, words flowing in a smooth, lulling rhythm. After a moment of watching him speak, I turn in the direction he faces.

The place where the fire started. Minion trails

coalesce around the side of my house, on what used to be the wall of the living room. Thick and heavy, they tell the tale of where the fire started. As my gaze scans the area, the trails darken, tiny pixels of color swirling into a shape.

The shape of a demon in its true form.

No human-like change for this demon. All the demons I've met looked like humans, their only physical giveaway their black eyes. This one looks like a medieval painting of demons. Red skin covers a huge, muscular body. Yellow horns protrude from its head. Gold necklaces wrap around his neck, while gem-encrusted rings cover his fingers. He's draped in what looks like a white silk toga with gold embroidery. Real gold threads, not the dyed kind.

His expression is pleasant enough, no gonna-kill-you-now glare. Whoever he is, he exudes wealth and power.

Smythe draws in a breath as he reaches the end of the spell. "Take a picture!"

"Where's your phone?" Yet another thing lost last night in the fire. At least phones can be replaced, contacts and pictures intact.

He pulls his out of his pocket, tossing it to me. "Hurry. I don't know how long this image will last."

I catch the phone, swipe the camera icon, and snap away, checking to ensure the image was caught digitally. Yep. Three pictures of the huge demon appear in all its glory, digitally captured for all time.

Or until someone hits the delete photo button.

Several seconds after I snap the last picture, the image starts to fade, becoming transparent until the shape drifts away into nothing.

"Who was that?" I toss the phone back to Smythe.

"I'm not sure. But we can find out. Come on. We also need to pick up a new phone for you and then we can go back to my place."

Picking up a new phone sounds almost as good as identifying the pretentious demon who targeted my house.

I glance at the spot where the minion died, the place the cleanup crew focused on earlier. The grass appears blood-free, no evidence of a fight to the death exists. Unless one considers the battle my house fought and lost. That battle they did nothing for, leaving the charred shell of my home as is.

"If the cleanup crew can repair doors, windows, and other destroyed stuff to hide a minion attack, can they rebuild my house?"

Smythe raises a brow. "There's a limit on how much one can repair. A door or window is one thing. Your house is too much. Besides, can you imagine all the memory scrubbing we'd have to do? Way too much. Get the check from the insurance and rebuild. Or better yet, move in with me."

I blink a couple of times. Were we serious enough to move in together? Hell, yeah. Did I even have to ask?

Okay, we're serious. As in long-term, he's mine and I'm his, serious.

But did I want to move to Boston?

"What about my job?"

"I can portal you in."

"Every day?"

He shrugs. "Sure. Why not?"

"Can I think about it?"

"Of course. I'm just throwing it out there."

"You caught me off guard."

One corner of his lip turns. "I caught myself off guard. Think about it. You don't have to decide now."

I give him a hug. "Ready to go pick me up a new phone and discover a demon's identity?"

"Always."

With a wave of his hand, coupled with words dripping with age and sounding suspiciously like Latin, he forms a portal. Together we step inside.

Chapter Twelve

Smythe grabs his laptop, sits at the table, and pulls up the picture of the demon on his phone. I take the chair next to him, peering over his shoulder. He types in the physical description of the demon, red skin and yellow horns, then scrolls through the images appearing on the screen.

I look closer. "Are those scanned drawings from old scrolls?"

The pen and ink sketches look ancient, the colors faded and cracked, the background a dull yellow-cream parchment. Some mage spent a good deal of time cataloguing the pictures in digital format.

"Yep. Librarians have been working for years digitalizing the ancient scrolls. They're about halfway through the library. Pictures of demons," he taps the screen, "were the first to be scanned."

"So what demon sent his minion to destroy my house?"

"One of these." His lips curve upward as he gestures at the laptop.

"Smartass."

The detailed drawings scroll by as we look at each one. The artists were skilled, much better than what I would do if forced to draw any of the demons I've fought. Finally, Smythe stops at a drawing that looks a lot like the demon's image from the spell he cast. He looks at his phone, then at the screen.

"Whatcha think?" He passes me the phone.

I look between the two pictures, the colored drawing and the photo snapped at my house. Almost identical.

"Looks the same to me. What demon is it?" Leaning closer to the laptop, I try to read the tiny print.

Smythe hits a couple of keys and the writing enlarges.

Mammon, the demon leader of greed. One of the most powerful demons in existence. He'd fought several *Justitians*. At once. And won.

Great. Just great.

"I wonder what he wants with you." Smythe raises a brow as he stares at me.

"No clue. As far as I know, I haven't pissed off the demon of greed. Or maybe I have. Maybe that's why I have nothing left. He had to take it from me."

"Not sure why he'd want a burned down house. No offense."

"Point taken. As you asked, why me?"

"We'll figure it out." A ding sounds on his computer and we both flinch.

"What's that?" I ask as he pulls up a different browser.

"I set a notification to let me know if the Agency accounts have been accessed. The accounts those minions were trying to get into?"

"Oh, yeah, those. You mean someone has dropped money into the Agency's account?"

"Yep." His fingers tap a dance against the keyboard. "I'm tracing it." A few seconds pass. "Huh. It's from a different financial advisor within the same company, but this time it's in Los Angeles."

"There's not a *Justitian* in LA, right?"

"Right. There probably should be with all the minion activity out there." He shakes his head. "Not sure what's going on. Why is this finance company making payments to the Agency? It doesn't make sense."

He leans back in his chair, brows drawn together as he rolls his fingers against his thigh. I watch him for a few moments before realizing I needed to call my insurance company and let them know about my lack of a house.

"You need me?"

He shakes his head.

"Okay, then, I'm going to call my insurance company."

After a long phone call where my agent takes down what happened, she takes my email and promises to send me a packet of information including a form I have to electronically sign and return. Once they have the signature, they can deposit a small check into my banking account to help with immediate expenses.

Easy enough. Except Smythe is on the only computer in the apartment.

"Can I borrow your laptop to check my email? I need to sign and return paperwork to the insurance company."

He glances up from the laptop. "There's another computer in the office you can use."

"The office?"

"More like the spare bedroom."

"You have two bedrooms?" What kind of idiot girlfriend am I not to notice he had two bedrooms?

Then again, we were usually a little busy with other things to take a tour of the apartment and I didn't stay over here long. He usually stayed at my place.

Still. I'm a certifiable moron.

He raises a brow and stares at me for a moment. I shrug.

"What can I say? I was too busy doing other things with you to notice?"

He grins. "Damn straight." He gestures to the hall. "It's right next to the bedroom."

I head that direction, feeling even dumber as I see what door he means. "I thought that was the linen closet."

He laughs. "Right. Like I have a linen closet. Help yourself to the computer. You might also want to call your credit card companies and have them reissue cards."

"I totally spaced on that. Thanks. I'll be in here for awhile."

****

An hour later, I've called the credit card companies, had them reissue cards, updated my driver's license online, and filled out the insurance paperwork. I lean back in the chair with a sigh.

What a mess. A complete and utter mess. My house is gone. Mammon, the demon of greed, sent a minion to kill me. My car and all my stuff are charred beyond recognition.

On the plus side, the credit card companies and insurance were Johnny-on-the-spot with reissuing cards and not giving me a hassle.

Most importantly, we were all alive. No injuries. No lung damage from smoke inhalation, thanks to

Smythe's protective bubble. And the world was down a minion, not like that particular stat would be around for long.

Life goes on. I will rebuild my house. Buy new possessions. All the things that count are with me now. Friends and family. Give me those two things and I can go on.

Enough thoughts. I want to see what Smythe has been doing while I've been in his office.

My mentor still sits at the table, eyes narrowed as he stares at the laptop. He drums his fingers on the table, rolling them pinky to thumb, pinky to thumb, pinky to thumb.

"What's up?"

His fingers pause as he looks at me. He shakes his head as he stretches, arms overhead, leaning the chair back on two legs. "Companies are paying the Agency. Big companies. Once I knew what to look for, it was easy to trace the companies' names to the owners. We're talking big names."

"Like who?"

He mentions several well-known billionaires who own huge, even better known, companies. My eyes widen.

"Why would they be paying the Agency? What are they getting in return?"

"No clue. I can't find outgoing expenses related to those accounts."

"I know we went over this before we knew who the companies were. One company in Dallas is one thing but this is way more than a single company. We need to figure out what's going on."

The two front chair legs drop with a muted thud

onto the carpet as Smythe leans forward. "It's like you said the other day—it looks like it's protection money."

"You mean like the mob does? You're calling the Agency a magical mob?"

He shrugs. "I don't know. That's the only thing I can think of because I know we aren't sending mages or *Justitians* to any of these companies to rid them of a demon or minion infestation. We have no other goods besides our magical ability so if that's not being used, then there's no legal reason for the payments."

"How long has this been going on? Maybe it's a secret thing? You know, like all those undercover top-secret government organizations?"

"Oh, listening to conspiracy theories again?" He grins.

I point a finger at him. "You know some of them exist."

His head tilts slightly to the side in a half-nod, a concession that maybe I'm right. Not that he'll admit it.

"To answer your question, the payments have been occurring regularly since the digital records were kept. Not sure how far back before then they go. Those records would be stored in the financial office in the Agency. If they haven't been destroyed after a certain period of time."

"Okay. So old records are unknown. But still, since digital records have been kept is an awful long time. You sure the Agency hasn't been sending a protection squad of demon fighting mages?"

"I can double check with Dad but I'm sure. That's not the way the Agency fights its battles."

"It's more reactive than proactive."

At least since I've been here. The one time they

tried to get proactive a couple of minions attacked the building in a helicopter, killing several mages, and injuring hundreds more.

"Being reactive has always worked in the past. There isn't a super secret mage fighting team either. If there was, I'd know about it."

"No offense, but are you sure about that?"

His eyes narrow. "Yes, I'm sure. I've made mistakes, but I'm higher up in this organization than my apartment floor level indicates. Dad always shared mission intel with me. He wanted me to move into his job when he retired." A shadow crosses his eyes.

I don't need to read his mind to know what he thinks. His expression says it all. David kept him in the loop until recently. Until behind the scenes machinations started. Until I came along.

I'm pretty sure David no longer tells Smythe everything happening at the Agency. Take, for instance, Samantha getting paid to set up minions to kill me. David knows more than he's letting on. He knows why she was paid to kill me. He might even have wanted her to do so, despite what he said.

David is an asshole. Unfortunately, he's also Smythe's father and it hurts Smythe to realize his dad is not a paragon of honesty.

Wait a minute. My thoughts tripped down the path of David, causing me to blank on the most important part of Smythe's sentence.

"You are being groomed to be the mage leader?"

He raises a brow. "You sound like you're surprised."

"Well, yeah." Heat slaps my cheeks, but I plow on anyway. In for a dime, in for a dollar. "No offense, you're powerful and all, but I can't see you wanting to lead everyone."

"What? You don't think I can lead?" Irritation laces his tone.

"No, no. I didn't say you can't. I said you don't seem like you want to. Am I wrong?" How could I miss something as important as my guy wanting to be in charge of all the mages?

He pauses, conflicting emotions written on his face. "Yes and no. Part of me wants it and the other isn't so sure."

"I think you'd be good at the job. You're honest." Unlike his father, the sentiment hanging behind my words.

A half-grin turns his lips. "Honesty might get you far in life but it's not the sole qualification to be a mage leader. Strength and battle ability are what they look for." The grin vanishes as his eyes grow haunted. "I'm strong but I've made mistakes. Big mistakes."

Jennifer. The *Justitian* he was guardian to, and his girlfriend, before me. She dumped him, and he was drunk off his ass when a minion attacked and killed her. Guilt still rides his conscious, undermining his confidence. Despite what he claims, he clearly hasn't forgiven himself.

"Everyone makes mistakes, Smythe. Look at mine." I killed a human. Okay, a couple but one of them barely counted as a human, even if he was my sperm donor. The other, Donny Merryweather, was seconds away from becoming a minion. I thought I could save Donny. Instead I killed him. Guilt rides me too, but you have to stop dwelling on it and move on or else you'll become stuck and grief-stricken.

And that's not a good place to be.

He sighs. "I know. I can't help the way I feel."

"I've said the same thing."

He barks a laugh. "Touché. So you have."

When he pauses, I take a step toward him, meaning to wrap him in a hug, but before I make it to him, someone knocks on the door.

I step back as he stands to open the door to Eloise and T.

"Hey!" I give them a smile. "Don't you normally portal on in?"

Eloise raises a brow as she walks to the sofa. "It's rude to portal in when Smythe is home."

"Teasing."

A hint of red tinges her pale cheeks. "Oh. In that case I thought I'd try for normal."

Smythe snorts. Right. Normal. Nothing about Eloise is normal.

"What did you find?" Smythe asks, gesturing T to sit next to Eloise.

Not that my twin needs the encouragement. I wink at him. He blushes. Yep. He and Eloise moved their relationship from I-like-you to do-me-now-baby. Finally.

Smythe takes his chair at the table, but turns it to face us, while I plop onto the recliner.

A wrinkle forms between T's brows as he glances at Eloise. "I saw a ghost again, but this time when she started talking about the Agency demon, I couldn't understand her. It made no sense. What's weird is I know I've talked to her before and understood what she said. I just can't remember."

"For some reason," Eloise glances at my twin,

"being at the Agency has caused the spell hiding the demon to work on T. I want to say he knew the demon's identity, but the memory is fuzzy to the point of not believing it."

A sudden headache throbs behind my eyes as I try to remember if T knew the identity of the demon. Did he? Did he not? Geez Louise, why can't I remember? "I hate this damn spell."

Everyone looks at me. I shrug.

"Seriously. I hate the spell the damn demon cast. I can't remember if T used to know the demon's identity. I can't remember if I knew the identity. No wonder you've known there was a demon at the Agency for years, Eloise, and not been able to do anything about it."

"We need a counterspell. Saying the demon's name or writing it down doesn't work."

I turn to Smythe. "Yeah. I'm pretty sure we've had this conversation before."

"Okay, since we're going in circles about it, let's move to something we do know and can talk about without headaches." Smythe looks at Eloise. "We cast the spell at Gin's and the demon's image who appeared was Mammon."

"Greed." Small wrinkles appear around Eloise's eyes. "Why would he attack Gin?"

T glares. "I take it Mammon is the demon of greed?" We all nod. "Eloise is right. What does he want with us? We don't have a lot of money."

"Mammon isn't solely about money." Eloise grabs his hand. "He's about greed of any kind. Wealth, power, information. But you're right. Why would he send a minion for Gin? Did you discover a treasure or something he wants?"

I laugh, unable to help myself despite the seriousness of the situation. "You think I'd be sitting here if I found a treasure? Nah, I have no idea why he wants me. Smythe and I were discussing it and didn't learn anything. Except how to talk in circles."

Eloise chews on her lip. "Mammon usually tries to kill those who have what he wants after he gets them to sign the wealth, or whatever, over to him. If you have nothing he wants, then you've upset him in some way."

"I've clearly more than upset him. He sent a minion to destroy everything I owned and try to kill me. He's after me. Gin Crawford. Me. Not the *Justitian*, but me. Why?"

The last time a demon targeted me as me was when I killed her regiment of demons. Actually, Smythe destroyed most of them, although I killed many. In retaliation, Jezebeth killed Blake, my friend with benefits. As far as I know, I haven't killed any of Mammon's minions.

Wait a minute. "Who did those minions belong to? The ones in the financial advisor's office?"

Smythe shrugs. "I don't know. Why?"

"Could we go back to the office and use the spell to determine the demon's identity? They were in a financial office. Maybe they belonged to Mammon? Maybe he's pissed we killed his minions?"

Smythe's eyes widen. "Eloise? Would the spell be able to track the demon this long after the minion was there? The minion trails would be gone now."

Eloise taps a finger against her lips. "I'm not sure. Casting the spell when the minion trails are still seen obtains the best results, but it wouldn't hurt to try."

I look at Smythe. "Wanna give it a shot?"

Smythe nods. "It's worth a try. We'll go once it's night."

Chapter Thirteen

The rest of the day passes with T trying to remember which of the many people he met had the highest potential of being the Agency's demon. Eloise had taken him to the library to study about ghost talkers but ran into what sounds like a bunch of people. Unlike last night, where we bypassed the landing room, opting to sneak into the building, she decided to introduce my twin as the Agency's newest ghost talker. According to Eloise, David was shocked T was my twin.

As if he didn't know I had a twin. And a twin with superhuman abilities to boot.

Right. I don't believe him.

On the other hand, I was surprised Chuck, Samantha, and a group of mages didn't blink an eye at T's abilities.

Could one of them be the Agency demon? If he remembers talking to them, does that make them demon free? How hidden is this demon?

By the end of the day my mind swims with confusion. I'm not the only one. We're all frustrated to be back at the beginning in discovering the demon's identity.

I'd call the day a wash except I managed to get credit cards replaced and the insurance called.

When dinnertime rolls around, we all take Smythe up on his offer to portal us to a pizza place in town.

Turns out to be the best pizza I ever ate. Maybe one day I can come to Boston when there's not a demon or two to catch and explore the city.

And the chances of that happening before I retire are slim to none.

Wait a minute. "Smythe, do *Justitians* ever retire?"

"We've been over this."

I face him. I almost say the words out loud except I don't want T to hear.

You said we wore the justitias *until we died.*

His jaw tenses. *Yes. I did.*

You're saying I won't retire.

He looks at his plate, his lips pressed tight. Which is answer enough.

A wave of sadness washes over me. I won't get to explore Boston without worrying about demons. I might not live another year.

Which shouldn't be a newsflash, but nonetheless is.

I swallow a sip of beer, trying to wash the bitter taste off my tongue. Regret. Regret I ever saw the *justitia.*

No, that's not entirely true. If I never slipped on the *justitia*, then I wouldn't have met Smythe. I wouldn't have killed evil.

I wouldn't have learned I possessed the ability to kill demons.

I would still be plain ol' Gin Crawford, nurse and struggling empath.

I've grown these last months. Grown into something better. A person who can be counted on to eliminate demonic entities. Not everyone can add that skill to their résumé.

So what if I come with a shortened lifespan. I kick

ass. And because I kick ass, I'll find a way to retire and explore one of America's oldest cities. If it's the last thing I do.

T snaps his fingers in front of my face, his foot nudging mine under the table. "Hey, sis. Wake up. What's the answer?"

"The answer?"

"Smythe said you guys have been over the retirement thing. What's the answer?"

"Oh. Sorry. I got thinking about something else. Retirement happens when you get a lot older than what I am now." I make sure all the barriers in my mind are up and strong, so he doesn't see my probable lack of making it to retirement age.

He gets mad enough knowing I fight demons. Knowing I won't live long would cause him to blow a proverbial gasket, or maybe a real one. Neither of which I want to see.

Eloise clears her throat. Not being a dummy, she understands why I'm trying to distract my brother.

"I'll go with you to Dallas. Maybe if I lend a hand with the demon-identification spell it will work."

I glance around the half-empty restaurant and drop my voice to a whisper. "Can you say that in here?"

Her lips twitch. "Do you think they can hear our conversation?"

I open my lips to say, *yeah I do*, but shut my mouth as a thought pops into my mind. I glance at T who shrugs. Smythe chuckles.

"You cast a spell, so no one can hear us."

Eloise grins. "You're smarter than you seem."

"Gee, thanks."

"It happens occasionally."

I glare at my laughing twin. He laughs harder. Brothers.

Smythe pats my hand. "Don't pay them any attention."

"Don't worry. I'm not." A smile creeps across my lips as happiness crawls through my veins, filling me with a sense of peace. Family and friends. Who could ask for more?

****

Eloise's portal drops us into the darkened financial advisor's suite in Dallas. Smythe casts a quick spell to turn off the alarm and erase our presence on the security cameras. We then walk down the hall to the office where I killed one of the minions.

Smythe and Eloise theorized since I chatted with the minion in this office, there might be a better chance of the spell working. And this office was not walled by glass like the waiting room at the front of the suite, which meant people in the hallway couldn't see us.

While a spell covered our tracks on the cameras, blinking ourselves out of existence from the casual passerby took more effort than Smythe or Eloise could produce and still cast the demon identification spell. Cleanup crews contained more than two mages for a reason.

T and I stand in the hallway outside the office as Eloise and Smythe cast the spell. Like at my house, a wavy image appears, only this time the demon appears more transparent than solid, faded like a picture left too long in the sun. However, the flickering image proves Smythe and Eloise were right about using this location to cast the spell.

I squint as the image comes in focus. Yellow horns

adorn a red scaly skinned demon. The same demon who appeared at my house.

Mammon. The demon of greed.

At least his minions breaking into a financial advisor's office made sense. More sense than why he wanted to destroy my house.

"Did the spell work?" Eloise looks toward Smythe.

"Yep. The image is faded, but there."

"Who is it?" T steps closer to the wavering, transparent demon.

I cross my arms and lean against the doorjamb. "Mammon. The leader of the greed demons."

"The same demon who sent the minion to burn down your house." Smythe glares at the transparent image.

T glances at the demon then to me, one brow raised. "Why? Why us?"

I shrug. "Don't know. Why would a greed demon want to kill me? I don't possess enough stuff for the leader of the greed demons to get all jealous and try to take what little I own. And he didn't try to steal my things, he destroyed them while trying to off me. Smythe and I couldn't figure it out."

"Two demons we are unsure about." Eloise shakes her head. "One of his motives and the other of their identity."

Greedy, greedy, greedy, chants my *justitia. Greedy, greedy, greedy.*

If you aren't going to tell me who it is, then shut up!

The *justitia* pauses before emitting what comes across my nerves as an exasperated sigh. *Can't tell. Need counterspell.*

I know we need it. If we knew what the spell was, do you really think we'd be standing here instead of tracking down the damn demon?

Call Zagan.

Right. Smythe would kill me. He doesn't want me to have anything to do with Zagan. Besides, I've never called him. He's always come to me.

The *justitia* pauses. *Go relieve yourself.*

You mean go to the bathroom?

Yes. Bathroom. The thing draws out the word as if it's never pronounced it before. *Say you need go bathroom. Call Zagan. Get spell. Don't tell mage.*

I straighten. Only to realize everyone stares at me. "Sorry. I was trying to remember where the restroom was in this place. Anyone know?"

Eloise shakes her head. T shrugs. A thoughtful expression drifts across Smythe's face. Never a good sign. Did he read my mind and eavesdrop on my conversation with the *justitia*? Could he even listen in on our conversation?

"I thought I saw one by the break room." Smythe points in the direction.

"Thanks. I'll be right back. Drank too much beer."

Hopefully Smythe's lie detector was on the fritz tonight.

I hightail it down the hallway to the one-seater next to the break room. Just like Smythe said.

After flipping the lock, I lean against the door and close my eyes.

Okay, justitia. *How do I call Zagan?*

Let me speak.

Like it does sometimes when we're fighting, it takes control of my body. I open my eyes, watching in the mirror as my lips move, as words I could never hope to speak on a good day roll off my tongue. Ancient words. Words dripping with a taste of evil, with a hint of darkness. Chills spring across my limbs as the scent of sulfur fills the room.

The *justitia* shakes a greeting against my wrist, its happiness a rush of pleasure along my nerves. Black fog swirls between me and the mirror, the stench of rotten eggs permeating my senses as my eyes water.

Part of me wants to run, the primeval part of my brain telling me to hide from this dangerous night creature. The other part of me wants to throw myself into his muscular arms, to give him a welcoming hug.

Which puts me halfway to insanity.

Instead of fleeing or hugging, I give the demon a finger-waggle. "Hi ya, Zagan."

Despite his business casual white button-down and black trousers ensemble, the demon's expression could stop a raging fire. Or maybe cause said fire. His black eyes glitter with more attitude than a teenager on a bad day. I take a step back or try to. Seeing how I'm against the door to begin with, my run-away attempt goes nowhere.

"To what do I owe the pleasure?"

Pleasure isn't the correct word for what he's clearly feeling, but I appreciate his attempt at politeness.

I swallow. Straighten my shoulders. I wanted him here. Too late to wish otherwise.

"I have a problem."

One black brow rises. "Oh? Do tell. And while you're at it, explain how you called me. You shouldn't be able to do so."

I hold out my *justitia*-covered wrist and give it a little shake. "Here's the how."

His eyes widen. "You can speak to each other?"

Surely he knew that already. "Yes." I refuse to explain. He created the damn bracelets. He should know the entity in them could talk to their host *Justitian*. "Back to my problem. We need a way to erase the effects of a forget-me spell."

"We?"

"Me, Smythe, Eloise, and T."

Black eyes focus on my face. An unstoppable shiver gives me a little shake. A lump forms in my throat and I swallow it away to continue answering Zagan's question.

"We're trying to discover the identity of the demon who has invaded the Agency. But the demon cast a spell to make us forget their identity. I'm told the counterspell is one a demon knows. You're a demon. I'm hoping you could help." I swallow again and offer him a grin.

"You are?" Both brows rise. "You called on me to help you? Does this mean you have given our relationship a second thought?"

"Relationship?" What the hell is the demon talking about now? "You mean our," I clear my throat, "friendship?"

He speaks in a slow cadence, as if convinced of my lack of intelligence. "The relationship I refer to is the one we should have since you wear my mark."

"Oh." I straighten while shaking my head. No way am I becoming his servant. "In that case, nope. No relationship between us, buddy."

He smiles, the tips of his white teeth showing.

"You called me buddy. You are leaning toward wanting to become my servant in truth." At my start of a protest, he holds up a hand. "Very well. You can believe what you want, but I know the truth. Now then"—once again he rolls over my meager attempt at a protest—"this demon. Who told you I possessed a remedy to a forget-me spell?"

I swallow. I swear one of these days I will convince the big, bad demon I will never be his servant. Clearly today is not that day. Which means I need to answer his question in order to get his help. "Eloise."

His grin grows wide, his black eyes sparkling with an unholy glee. "Ah. Eloise. And how is she today?"

"Fine. She's fine. Are you going to give me the spell or not?" I narrow my eyes to let him know I mean business, to try to hide a frisson of fear behind aggression.

"I need to cast this spell on you." His nose wrinkles. "And your friends. I cannot cast it from afar and expect it to work. It must be placed on each individual for maximum effectiveness."

So much for Smythe not learning about me calling Zagan for help. I'd hoped the spell could be cast from a distance and then Smythe, Eloise, and T would never realize I'd talked to the demon of deceit.

I sigh. I'm not afraid of Smythe chewing out my ass. Really. I'm not. Shit. Who am I fooling? My gaze shifts to the side. The things I do to keep humans safe from demons. I swallow. "Okay. But they won't be happy to see you."

He shrugs, a hint of amusement mingled with a large dose of nonchalance crossing his face. "When are they ever?"

Chapter Fourteen

Zagan follows me to where the others stand talking in the office and clears his throat. Which, of course, snaps all attention to us. Eloise's eyes widen as if she can see the demon standing in the doorway. With a not so subtle movement, she steps in front of T, who appears too busy staring at the demon to notice her protective stance. T's breath sucks into his lungs on a hiss.

Smythe's narrowed gaze and aura of anger slam into me with a physicality causing me to stumble back a foot. Regaining my balance, I speak before Smythe voices his dislike of everything Zagan. "Zagan's going to help us get rid of the forget-me spell."

If possible, my mentor's black brows drop even lower. I straighten my spine, giving him my best nurse's glare, the one reserved for disobedient patients.

"Eloise," Zagan takes a step toward the healer, hand outstretched as if to shake hers, effectively breaking the palpable tension between me and Smythe. I'm willing to bet the more-astute-than-I-give-him-credit-for demon did it on purpose. "How nice to see you again."

Eloise nods, keeping her hand by her side. "Zagan."

The demon drops his hand so as not to look stupid with it hanging in mid-air. T finally removes his gaze from the demon, notices Eloise stands in front of him, and moves to her side. His eyes narrow, all semblance of awe vanishing the longer he stares at the demon. Zagan's gaze hops between me and my twin as if comparing our differences.

"Gin." Smythe draws out my name, aggravation written in the undertones.

Yep, as I thought, he's none too happy with me. He can deal with it. If we want to discover the Agency demon's identity, we need all the help we can get. Even if that help comes from Hell.

I shrug. "We needed help."

You called a demon? T's incredulous voice echoes in my mind.

He can help us.

Can you trust him?

Can I? It depends. Do I trust him to help us in this matter? Yes, I do. Do I trust him not to try to convince me by whatever means to become his servant in truth? Nope, not at all. As I said. It depends. A fact I conveniently leave out of our conversation. *In this, yes.*

All right, then. T's narrowed eyes relax. *Strange times call for strange deals.*

Unlike my twin, Smythe remains unconvinced. No surprise there. He was brought up to believe all demons were evil and could not be trusted. "I told you not to call him. We can't trust him. For all we know, he'll say a spell to make us believe he's God."

Zagan releases a noisy breath, a cross between a laugh and a harrumph, his opinion clearly in opposition to my mentor. "Don't be ridiculous. No spell would make you believe I was God. Your master, maybe, but not God."

"Same thing." Smythe crosses his arms. "We don't need your help."

Mages. So stubborn even in the face of reality.

"Oh, yes we do." I grab Zagan's clothed arm. "We need you to cast the spell."

"No—"

"Aidan." Eloise touches Smythe's arm, interrupting him. "If we are to find this demon, we need Zagan's help."

"But—"

She shakes her head. "No buts. Gin trusts him to cast this spell. Let's agree to let him."

White lines bracket Smythe's mouth as he presses his lips together. For once Zagan remains quiet, letting my mentor reach the conclusion the rest of us have already reached: we need the demon's help.

After a long, tension-filled pause, Smythe's eyes narrow on Zagan. "How do we know you'll say the correct spell?"

Zagan offers a shiver-inducing smile. Way to ensure trust, demon. Making the big, bad mage cringe in his shitkickers is not the way to convince him he needs your help. But then Zagan speaks, his words laced with sincerity.

"I want this demon gone as much as you do. If I do not cast the spell, then the demon will not be identified, and my desire will not come to fruition. You can trust me."

Smythe's brows rise for a brief moment. "You are willing to kill another demon, one of your brethren?" Judging by his tone, he didn't believe me when I told him Zagan wanted to kill several powerful demons in order to gain control of Hell.

"Are all humans worth living?" Zagan mirrors Smythe's glare of disdain. "Of course not. Neither are all demons. Are you actually complaining about eliminating a demon? You? A mage?"

Smythe's jaw tightens. Eloise white-knuckles his arm.

"Zagan," she meets the demon's gaze. "We accept your assistance in this matter."

He tilts his head toward her. "As you and Gin wish."

Smythe opens his mouth to protest, his words dying on his lips as Zagan begins speaking in a language as old as time.

Twisted words fall off his lips, striking a cadence deep inside my soul, eliciting a shiver of desire. Demonese. Since it's the native language of my *justitia*, I understand the words.

Not that I could ever hope to pronounce them. At least not without the *justitia* taking control of my body.

As Zagan continues to speak the spell, the words turn into droplets of light surrounding him like an aura. He gathers the light into his hands as he chants. With a loud cry, he shoves the white light toward us, the bright wave crashing over everything in the room, surrounding all in the brilliance of the spell.

Tingles spread throughout my limbs as the light passes over me, through me. As he continues casting the spell, the light draws back into his body. With a tiny *pop*, it vanishes inside him. Zagan stops speaking and nods once.

"You are now protected from the forget-me spell."

I glance at my hands, twisting them back and forth, ensuring they continue to be attached to my wrists.

Which they are, despite the pins-and-needles feeling slithering across my skin. A full-body shiver slides down T's body as he stares wide-eyed at the demon. He's not the only one with the nonplussed expression.

My brain whirls as it tries to remember the identity of the Agency demon. Nada. Zippo. Nothing appears. I glance to the others, hoping to see an *ah-ha* look on their face. Nope. Not happening.

Damn it. Did the spell not work?

Giving my hands one last shake, I speak to Zagan. "Thank you, but I still don't know who the demon at the Agency is."

Zagan rolls his eyes. "Of course you don't. You forgot."

"But your spell—"

"Will only protect you when you run into the demon. Then you can see them for who they are. Thanks to my spell."

"We appreciate the help." Despite his tense jaw, Smythe manages to pull politeness out of his back pocket. Something tells me at the moment he's more thankful he's not bowing down to worship Zagan than for the counterspell.

"Thank you, Zagan." Eloise tilts her head in his direction.

"Yeah, thanks." T glances at me for a second, wondering if he needed to offer more thanks to the demon of deceit.

I give him a quick head shake. No more thanks needed. Especially since we now need to either find T's Agency ghost or walk around until we meet the demon haunting the Agency halls. Again.

On the plus side, we've been given the spell to

identify the demon. So what if it requires more effort to get results than I thought?

"Since, out of the goodness of my heart, I have accomplished what you requested, I will depart." Zagan turns to me, his black eyes focusing a bit too intensely on my face, as if trying to worm his way into my thoughts.

Good luck, buddy.

As if he can read my mind, one side of his lips kicks upward into a lopsided grin. "I will see you later." He winks as he circles a hand over his head, vanishing into an overhead portal.

A breath I didn't realize I held rushes out, along with half the metaphorical steel holding my spine upright. I did it. I called a demon to help us learn the identity of another, eviler demon.

The sense of pride lasts only for a second, until Smythe opens his mouth.

"What the hell, Gin?" Smythe takes a step toward me, anger creasing lines in his face, his body seeming to grow with righteous indignation.

At one time in my life, his anger would have had me cringing. Now, though, I know no matter how pissed off he gets, he'll never hurt me. Unfortunately, my twin doesn't feel the same.

T steps in front of Smythe, all glare and testosterone, in a posture of protection. "Leave her alone."

Uh-oh, if I don't diffuse the situation, my twin and my lover are going to come to blows. Or at least it appears that way. I step to their side, placing a hand on each of their chests.

"Okay, okay. Calm down. Both of you." I turn to

Smythe. "I'm sorry to upset you, but we needed the counterspell. According to Eloise, there is no other way." I shake my head as he tries to speak. "No. As much as it pains me to say this, we needed Zagan. I know you don't like it, but what's done is done."

"I'm not convinced using a demon to take down another demon is the correct thing to do."

"It's Zagan."

"I know. That's the problem. You can't see straight where he's concerned."

"Aidan." Eloise pats his arm. "I agree with Gin. We needed a demon and Zagan was willing to help. The end result is worth working with him if it means bringing down the Agency demon. The demon in the Agency is more of a threat than Zagan."

After a long pause, some of the tension drains from Smythe, causing T's puffed up anger to deflate. Double good.

"Fair enough." Smythe takes a step away from T. "I suppose you have a point. We do need to stop the Agency demon. Whoever it is has been there long enough. But I'm still not convinced Zagan doesn't pose a large threat."

"I never said he didn't." A corner of Eloise's lip turns up. "I said he wasn't as big of a threat as the Agency demon."

Smythe returns her half-grin. "Now that we have that settled. Let's go back to the Agency and see if we can determine who this demon is. The quicker we can get rid of them, the better. Eloise, would you like to do the honors, or do you want me to?"

As an answer, Eloise opens a portal. She winks at Smythe as she grabs T's hand and together they are swallowed into the in-between. Smythe grabs my hand and we follow them into the portal.

Chapter Fifteen

We land in Smythe's apartment, another round of tingles spreading through my body as I step out of the portal. Despite the tingles, I like avoiding the landing room. It's sneaky and underhanded.

Maybe that's a problem.

Nah. To catch a demon we need the occasional sneakiness.

The portal snaps closed. Smythe paces to the kitchen, his black shitkickers stomping the hell out of the carpet. So much for him agreeing we were correct in getting Zagan's help.

"Water?" He holds up a glass.

I shrug. "Sure."

Smythe fills the glasses from a filtered pitcher he grabs out of the fridge and passes them out to us. Once we sit, he starts talking.

"Eloise, you and T should scope out the building tomorrow. See if you can find the ghost. Or the demon. Gin and I will also look around the place." He takes a sip of water, then points the glass at Eloise. "You wouldn't happen to know why payments are coming into the Agency, would you?"

"Payments?" Little lines form around Eloise's eyes.

"Why's that so strange?" T asks. "They have money dripping off the ceilings. I'd think someone would be paying them."

Eloise and Smythe stare at my twin as if he sprouted horns. Eloise shakes her head.

"No, payments should not be coming in to the Agency. The Agency gains its money from investments," Eloise says.

"That's what I thought too, until I did some investigating." Smythe drums his fingers against his thigh. "Regular payments are coming in from a variety of different financial institutions. A little more digging showed the payments are from huge companies and their owners." He mentions the name of a billionaire who owns one of the companies.

"That's odd."

"Yeah, that's what I thought. I need to do some more digging but even if I discover who all the accounts belong to, the bigger question is why they are paying the Agency."

"Hush money," T says.

"That's my thought." Twins think alike. "Like a mob payoff. The Agency holds something over these companies and they're paying them to keep it quiet."

"Gin, the conspiracy theorist." Smythe grins and shakes his head.

I raise my glass to him. "Maybe, but we're talking about the Agency. This whole place is shadier than the middle of a forest in the dead of night."

Eloise chokes out a chuckle. "I like that comparison. Aidan, I will leave the hacking and discovery to you. You are much better at those types of things than I. Tomorrow, T and I will hunt for the ghost."

"And maybe hit the library for more info on ghost

talkers?" T actually sounds excited about studying. *Probably for the first time in his life.*

He glares at me. *Not the first time, sis.*

I cover up my grin with a long sip.

"We can do that too." Eloise pats his hand while looking at a yawning Smythe. "Sleepy, Aidan?"

Red tinges his cheeks. "Sorry. Yeah, I am. I'm ready for bed."

A mental image drifts into my mind of exactly what he wants to do to and with me when we crawl into his bed. Heat warms my core, flushes my cheeks.

T clears his throat. "Yeah, me too. Ready to go?" He grabs Eloise's hand.

She smiles. I don't need to use my empath abilities to know what's on their agenda for the evening.

T takes her glass and puts it with his in the sink. After hugs and "good nights" they leave Smythe and me alone. Smythe locks the door and turns to me with a predatory grin on his lips.

"Ready for bed?"

Putting a swing in my hips, I walk toward the bedroom, letting actions speak louder than words.

****

"This was a bad idea."

Smythe glances at me, one brow raised, silent talk for "it needs to be done so shut up and get to it." He might have a point but then again, after a couple of hours of walking up and down each hallway at the Agency searching for the demon and coming up with nada, I'm sticking with my original thought. This was a bad idea.

Sure, it sounded good last night and this morning. Right up until about thirty minutes ago when I realized there was no demon occupying the esteemed Agency today. Couldn't be. We'd have caught the damn thing by now.

The highlight of the day was the phone call from the detective about my house. The preliminary report says the fire was caused by tampering with the gas line to the house.

Duh. I could've told them that. Along with who did it, but they wouldn't believe me if I said a minion blew up my house in an effort to kill me. Taking a trip to Blue Shores is not anywhere on my to-do list.

So I said the right things, coating my words with the appropriate amount of shock and surprise. The detective responded with the typical, we'll keep you posted, and hung up.

Since then, Smythe and I have canvassed hallways and opened conference rooms of the Agency building, scouting for a demon who refuses to appear. My feet hurt. My *justitia* continues to be creeped out, jittering every now and then, its eerie voice wending through my nerves.

Demon?

I used to believe the thing hated the Agency because of the white noise coating the building, courtesy of spells keeping it hidden from human eyes. Now I realize my faulty thinking. It's not white noise making the thing jittery, it's an actual freaking demon.

In all the times I've come here, despite the entity's questioning the location of a demon, it's only once turned into a sword, and that was right before minions attacked the building. Like some sort of a premonition. Or malfunction, which is what I thought at the time.

Could it have sensed a demon in the conference

room right before the minions attacked? My forehead hurts as I think back to that day. Almost everyone employed by the Agency from all over the world came to that meeting. Maybe the demon came too.

Great. A place to start with over a thousand potentials vying for recognition in the game of who's the demon. Yeah. We can narrow down the identity in no time flat.

I roll my eyes and shake my head as I continue to plod along beside Smythe. We're no closer to discovering the demon than we were when we started this exercise in futility this morning.

And we had the audacity to believe a jaunt along every hallway would magically make the demon appear?

Yeah. As I said. This was a bad idea.

Although I am getting a bunch of steps on my phone's health app. Maybe the thing will stop notifying me about my lack of exercise. It could happen.

"We should go see Dad."

Now it's my turn for the raised brow, what-the-hell expression. "Why? He's yet to believe anything you tell him about the corruptness of this place. No offense, but what if he's in on knowing who the demon is?" Because if I had to pick one person at the Agency who had their hands all over the demon, it would be David.

Not only is the man a turd of epic proportions, but he's also as shady as a moonless night. But Smythe loves him, so I keep my thoughts to myself. Or try to. It's not a secret I'm not a fan of his dad.

Smythe sighs, stops, and leans against the wall. "That's what I'm afraid of. I don't want it to be true, but something's been off with Dad for a while. Even before you became a *Justitian*. I wrote it off to other things until you started pointing it out. Now it's impossible to look back over the years and discard all those small things that add up to a large amount of evidence." He crosses his arms, leans his head against the wall, and looks at the ceiling as if the thing holds answers. "I don't know what to think."

Your dad stinks like rotten trash. Check me out, keeping the thought to myself. At least I try to. Smythe has a nasty habit of popping into my mind when I least expect it. I school my face into portraying a neutral expression.

Judging by his head shake, I'm not as successful as I'd hoped. One of these days I'll get it right.

"If you think it would help, then go talk to him. I'll go back to your apartment. Maybe he'll tell the truth if I'm not around." Not likely, but it sounds better than, *I really, really, really don't want to see your dad.*

"I need more evidence. Telling him we know there's a demon but don't know their identity, won't endear him to our cause. We need proof. We need the demon to appear, so we know who it is."

"I'm not thinking the thing's going to poof in front of us with a 'howdy.' And walking around isn't working. On the plus side, I now know the uncomfortable feeling my *justitia* has every time it comes here isn't because of the white noise. It's because of the demon."

Smythe snaps his gaze off the ceiling and onto me, blue eyes sparkling with hope. "Do you think it knows who the demon is?"

"It hasn't said anything to me."

Greedy, greedy, greedy, the *justitia* chants, its eerie

voice echoing in my mind. *Greedy, greedy, greedy.*

I straighten. Could it be its trying to tell me the demon's identity? *Are you saying the demon at the Agency is Mammon?*

Greedy, greedy, greedy.

Is that a yes?

Greedy, greedy, greedy.

Right. Because saying a simple, three letter word appears to be beyond the scope of my *justitia.*

"What is it?"

"My *justitia* keeps chanting, 'greedy, greedy, greedy,' over and over." A remembrance creeps into my brain and I suck in a gasp of air. "It's said this before. I can't remember when, though." The memory tries to appear, tries to solidify in the way wispy vapor forms over a cooling lake, finally giving up and dissipating in the sun.

When did the *justitia* chant the same words?

Smythe's eyes widen. "Is it trying to say Mammon is the demon here? Is he the one we're trying to catch?"

"I don't know. I can't get it to say 'yes.' It just keeps chanting the greedy refrain."

"It makes sense if that's who it is. Mammon sent his minions to the financial advisor's office in Dallas, which corresponds to a payment to the Agency. What if we're not tracking two demons but one?"

I glance up at a golden chandelier, a good example of all the money dripping off this building. The Agency rolled in the dough, rolled more than investments and selling antiquities provided. Not that I ever see any of it in my banking account. Oh no, they refuse to pay *Justitians*—or maybe it's just this particular *Justitian*—for doing their job and killing off demons and minions.

They have to have another golden chandelier for their hallway.

Nope, I'm not jealous. In the least. Right. I'm such a freaking liar.

"Good point." My head nods in a slow up and down motion as I reply. "Look around. Look at how rich and fancy this place is. For no good reason. Do golden chandeliers really help mages and *Justitians* improve their fighting skills? I doubt it. If Mammon is the Agency demon and also the reason why a bunch of payments from billionaires are occurring at regular intervals, then it makes sense why everything in this place yells 'hello, wealth.' "

Smythe mimics my slow moving bobblehead. "The more I think on it, the more it makes sense. The two demons we hunt are one and the same. I'm calling our suspicion correct: Mammon is the Agency demon."

"Well, we're halfway there. Now we need to figure out who he is and how he's hidden himself for almost a century."

"And his end goal."

"Geez, Smythe, everyone knows a demon's end goal. World domination. Subjugation of humans. I guess he thinks that goal is better reached by taking over the Agency."

Creases form around his eyes. "What if he has taken over the Agency?"

"You mean he worked his way up from whatever he came in as?" A scary thought.

"Or he's enthralled humans to do his bidding."

An even scarier thought.

"Would that explain why Eloise felt a demonic presence over the years but never could identify exactly which person it was?"

"Maybe. If the demon enthralled a human but not for long."

"I didn't think demons could possess a human unless the human was open to the possession. Like when we hunted Agramon." I shiver at the thought of the fear demon. Thank god he was no more. "He tried to possess good people and they killed themselves."

"That was a possession. Enthralling a human without making the human its servant or minion can be done, but the demon would have to be extremely strong and expend a bunch of energy. Which is why they seldom enthrall."

"They leave enthralling to vampires, huh?" My chuckle induces an eye roll.

"You know as well as I, vampires don't exist."

"Yeah, yeah. Couldn't resist. Demons can really enthrall humans without making them their servants or minions?" Now that was a scary thought.

"Only if they're willing to expend a bunch of energy for short-term effects."

"Unlikely, right? I might not have passed Demonology 101, but even I know demons would rather go for the long-term goals of a human servant or minion." Except for Agramon, but that demon was a whole different class of scary-ass. "And while a demon walks these 'esteemed' halls, I've yet to see a minion running around loose. Someone's *justitia* would've fired into a sword at some point over the years."

"A *justitia* should've fired in the presence of the demon. Why didn't one?"

"Mine did, at that meeting." I don't have to elaborate. There was only one meeting prefaced by 'that' and everyone knew which one it was.

Minions flying a helicopter to attack the Agency only happens once.

"No one else's turned into a sword until the minions appeared in that helicopter. I always thought yours malfunctioned." A thoughtful expression crosses his face, a memory or an explanation? Since he fails to elaborate, I continue the conversation.

"Clearly it didn't. Of course, the fact we know now it wasn't a malfunction doesn't help. There were like over a thousand people at that meeting."

"Not quite that many." He shakes his head.

"Whatever. The point is, there were a bunch of people there so even if we assume my *justitia* sensed a demon and reacted accordingly, it doesn't help us. The demon could've been any number of people."

"True—"

Whatever he wants to say next is cut off by my ringing phone. Holding up a hold-on-a-minute finger, I yank the thing out of my back pocket, look at the caller ID—why is Blue Forest Emergency calling?—and swipe to answer.

"Hello?"

"Gin!" My spine straightens as Will shouts my name in a tone filled with panic. "A couple of minions are attacking the Emergency Department! Can you come?"

Background noises filter through the phone, loud voices, screams, what sounds like a slamming door. Will draws in a gasp.

Oh my god. "Where in the department are you? Are you okay?"

As if I touch him, his fear infuses me, racing my

heart, clouding my thoughts.

"I'm in a patient room with the door locked but I don't know how long the door will hold. They're knocking down the doors. You have to get here fast!"

A hitch in my voice keeps me from replying. Smythe saves me from answering, holding out his hand for the phone, clearly listening in to our conversation. Which is just as well. Him listening in means I don't have to repeat what Will said.

"We'll be there in a minute." With a quick glance my way, he starts running toward the elevator, me following several strides behind due to his long legs. "Is there someone in the room with you?"

By the time I catch him, the elevator has arrived and he's waiting for me, holding the door with his foot. As soon as I step inside, he pushes the floor for the landing room.

"Okay, keep the line open. I'll wipe her mind when we arrive." He pauses as Will's tinny voice asks a garbled question. "Yes, we'll be there in less than a minute. Hold on. Don't hang up."

The elevator doors slide open and we dash down the hall to the landing room. Smythe yanks open the door and holds his free hand toward the corner of the room, the spot where all entrances and exits occur. The row of teenage mages glances at us as Smythe speaks his portal forming words. Once the portal opens, he grabs my hand, yanking me into the icy depths of the in-between.

Chapter Sixteen

A couple of seconds later, the portal spits us out where Will huddles beside a wide-eyed, pale-faced elderly woman in a hospital gown. Who becomes even more wide-eyed and pale-faced as we step into the room. No surprise. Seeing a couple of people suddenly appear in a gust of deceptively warm air tends to do that to a person.

It probably doesn't help that my *justitia* chooses that moment to morph into a sword.

Smythe hands me my phone, which I slip into my pocket as he steps to the woman's side. He touches her arm. "You've had a bad dream. Go back to sleep and everything will be okay."

The woman's eyes narrow. "Sonny, I might be old but I ain't stupid. If this is a bad dream, I'm your alcoholic uncle. And I don't drink."

Smythe wipes surprise off his face then pats her arm. "Sleep." This time he uses a larger dose of compulsion. The woman's eyes drift closed as tension relaxes from her body.

I want to ask why he didn't push compulsion into her the first time around, but more important things take precedent. Like looking Will over and confirming he appears uninjured. Thank god he seems okay. Freaked out, but physically okay. I squeeze his shoulder. One side of his lips turns in acknowledgement as he nods once.

"Thanks for coming."

"Happy to." I drop my arm while drawing in a deep breath.

Fighting time.

Smythe beats me to the door, his phone held against his ear as he whispers into it for the Agency to send backup from the cleanup crew and a couple of extra mages. One kickass *Justitian* and several mages should be able to destroy a few minions. Should being the operative word in the sentence.

Since he blocks the door, I wait until he ends the call and slips the phone into his back pocket, my nerves a jangling, eager mess. I'm ready to kick some minion ass.

Will waits by the patient as Smythe cracks open the door. Screams echo down the hall, a cacophony of panic and fear. Deep laughter chases the screams.

Damn minions.

Smythe yanks the door wide and I dart through the opening, heart pounding a fast rhythm. The metallic scent of blood hangs in the air. A shrill emergency alarm ululates, the normal ear-splitting wail mere background noise to a symphony of terror. Small lights high up on the walls flash a strobe pattern. A recorded voice tells us to leave the building immediately.

Right. A little hard to do with a band of evil minions blocking the exit.

My fellow employees huddle around the nurses' station, the central hub of the emergency department and the current location of two snarling minions. Two other minions block the nearby exit, swords held in front of their chests. Bodies litter the floor. Screams sound from the patient rooms. Red dots scatter along the periphery of my vision.

These people are good people. They're my friends, my coworkers, angels in the war on injury and disease. And these minions have the audacity to hurt them? To scare them? To kill them?

Fuckers are going down.

I stride toward the huddle of coworkers, my shoes thudding an incoming warning against the white linoleum. The sword catches the strobing alarm flashes, reflecting spots of bright light along the corridor.

I will kill these minions. Send what's left of their souls to rot in Hell. Vengeance is mine.

"Hey, boys." My voice carries over the alarm, screams, and rush of bodies attempting to flee, freezing the minions into a predatory stillness.

The four minions turn to me, shit-eating grins plastered on their faces.

"*Justitian.*" A tall, blond male—the leader terrorizing my coworkers at the nursing station—takes a step my direction. "We've been looking for you."

"Object achieved." I hold my arms out to my side. "What are you waiting for? Come and get me."

A couple of nurses poke their heads around the corner of the nursing station. Their gazes fall on me, almost as heavy as the minions' attention. Part of me feels like I'm showing off, exhibiting powers none of them could ever hope to possess. Will they still feel the same about me after I slaughter these minions? On the other hand, who the hell cares? Once the cleanup crew finishes scrubbing their memories, this whole fight will, in their minds, be non-existent.

The blond minion swings his sword—how the hell

did he get so close?—and I jump out of the way to avoid it. Unfortunately, I don't move fast enough and the blade slices across my upper arm.

Damn it. I really need to get out of my head and into the fight before I lose.

Then it won't matter what my coworkers think of me. I'll be dead.

I bring my sword across my chest, parry the minion's blow. Clattering blades join the cacophony of the wailing alarm as I back the minion into a corner.

Before I can strike a killing blow, another minion takes a swing at me. As if they realize ganging up on a *Justitian* is the only way to win the battle.

But I have a trick up my sleeve—more like throughout my nervous system—they don't know.

Can you give me super-speed?

A low chuckle sounds along my nerves, wends through my veins, sends power to my muscles. The eerie voice of the *justitia* echoes in my mind. *Me give speed. You kill minion. We defeat demon.*

Like before, a rush fills my limbs as the entity powers my movements. In a blur of motion, I spin, duck, swing, and parry as all four minions come at me at once. One gets in another slice. One aims a fist in my general direction with a hard blow catching me in the jaw.

I pinwheel to the floor on a wave of dizziness. Lucky for me, the *justitia* shuts down all my pain receptors. Unlucky for me, the entity can do little for the cuts and nothing for the room swirling a wild jig. I shake my head, trying to clear my vision. Stupid move. The room continues its tilt-a-whirl dance.

I shove to my feet as the minions advance,

operating on the theory that the *justitia* will power my movements even though I'm unable to see straight. And I'm right. The entity hisses in my head and then controls my sword arm so fast I have no idea what moves I'm making. Seeing as three minion heads roll across the formerly pristine white floor, I really don't care.

Dead minions trump powering my own body.

The last minion faces off with me, his expression a cross between surprise and anger. I pull my arm up to strike.

"No!" Smythe hollers at me, his screech pulling me out of the beginnings of super-speed. "We need to question him. He's the only one left."

Before I can retort with a pithy 'of course he's the only one left, I killed the rest', my gaze snags on five minion bodies stacked in a pile. Right. Remember all those screams from the rooms, Gin? Minions. Looks like the mages didn't wait for my blade to kill the demon's essence and took matters into their own hands.

Instead of being miffed the part of the demon animating the minion returned to its host, I'm glad they took care of business. Fewer minions are always a good thing.

I meet Smythe's gaze and nod, dropping my sword arm.

The minion's eyes widen as he looks between my mentor and me. For a second, I think the guy is going to bolt as his gaze hops around the ER as if looking for a quick exit.

It's then I notice the extra mages strategically placed at all the exits. Security guards stand next to them, eyes glazed, frozen in place, clearly under a spell.

My attention snaps back to the minion but not before I see my coworkers with the same glazed look as the guards.

I've never noticed the frozen humans on the rare occasions I've fought minions in front of them, but then again, a cleanup crew as well as a group of mages aren't normally present for my fights. On the plus side, freezing humans keeps them from needing excessive memory scrubbing.

I blink myself back to the here and now. No more tripping down rabbit trails while in the middle of a fight. Even if my fight has been paused.

I take a step toward the minion, then another, and another, until the wall halts his retreat. The flat of my blade presses against his throat.

"Drop your sword." He doesn't move, except for his shifting gaze darting to the enclosing mages. "Now!" I press deeper and his sword clatters to the floor as his eyes narrow.

Happy about his current circumstances is not how I would describe him. Pissed off was more his state of mind. Without warning, he grabs my arm, forcing the sword closer to my throat. Putting all my weight into a shove, I manage to move the sword an inch.

He glares. I snarl. Smythe knocks him upside the head, muttering words under his breath.

The minion drops to the floor.

"We don't have time for this shit." Smythe kneels beside the downed minion. "The cops are almost here, and the crew can't freeze them all. We need to get him out of here." He pulls the downed minion into a fireman's hold. "Come on, you and I need to leave."

"What about—" I gesture to my frozen coworkers.

The only one moving is Will, who stands in the doorway of the exam room, gaze meeting mine. The shocked expression frozen on his face strikes me as comical, although there's nothing funny about the situation.

Smythe hefts the minion into a more comfortable position. "The cleanup crew and other mages will take care of scrubbing memories and getting rid of the headless minions. Hurry, we need to leave. TaRhonda, Delores, come with me." He hollers at two mages.

"What about Will?"

"What about him?" Smythe speaks his portal forming words as two female mages, one with short, black, curly hair and one with long brown hair, step beside us.

I give Will another glance. He holds up one hand, mouthing the words 'thanks', his shocked expression morphing into determination as he glances at the carnage. I give him a nod and a wave before grabbing Smythe's arm and entering the portal. My friend appears fine and knows better than to speak of mages, minions, and portals to the cops. He'll be okay.

Chapter Seventeen

The lavender scent of the landing room greets us as we step out of the portal. A dull *beep-beep-beep* announces our arrival. Or maybe that of the minion. The teenage mages jump to their feet when they notice the minion Smythe carries. What do you know? They do move when a minion appears.

Of course, in this instance the minion is unconscious and escorted by three mages and a *Justitian*, so an exhibition of the teenagers' magical abilities remains non-existent.

"What happened?" One of the teenagers asks.

"Captured during a fight." TaRhonda answers as she follows Smythe out the door, leaving the monitors of the landing room curious.

I'm curious too. Where are we taking a minion? The last captured minion brought into the Agency was tortured someplace in this building. I shiver. Torture doesn't sit well with me even if it occurs to a demonic entity. I'd rather chop their heads off or stab them in the heart. Clean and easy. Well, maybe not so clean, but definitely not torturous.

Hopefully I won't be expected to participate in withdrawing info from the minion in any manner other than talking.

Smythe leads us to the elevator where TaRhonda pushes the down button. Once the elevator arrives, we enter, and once again, she pushes the button to the basement. Of course. Where else would you put the minion dungeons? The penthouse suites?

The elevator opens into a hallway featuring dull, khaki walls and off-white linoleum floors, none of the opulence of the rest of the building apparent in the basement. Our shoes thud and squeak against the floor as we continue to follow Smythe down the hall. He stops outside a non-descript door at the end of a long row of doors and waits until Delores opens it.

The room contains a metal desk and two chairs, similar to the ones seen in police procedurals on TV. Shackles dangle from the bolted-to-the-floor table. Smythe drops the minion onto the chair in front of the chains and snaps the table cuffs to the unconscious minion's wrists.

"Ready for him to talk?" Delores asks while Smythe parks it in the extra chair.

"Yep."

TaRhonda stands to one side of Smythe, while Delores walks to the minion, stopping a foot from where he slumps in the chair.

She speaks a spell, pushing her hands in the minion's direction. A shiver shakes through his limbs. He releases a moan as he raises his head, blinking his eyes several times as if the movement helps him wake.

And here I thought Smythe threw a punch hard enough to knock the minion out cold. His punch apparently contained a spell. Which I should have realized since he muttered words under his breath while knocking out the minion.

Sometimes I wonder about myself.

I lean against the wall to the right of the door, try to

cross my arms, and think better of it as I almost slice myself on the *justitia's* sword. Not a good look. Luckily no one notices my near miss.

Except the minion. A smile creeps across his lips as he stares at me as if I'm his next meal.

Fat chance. He's surrounded by mages and shackled to the table. No way is he escaping. Minions don't possess magic. Super-strength, sure. Magic, not even a little.

"Who is your demon?" Smythe asks.

The minion shrugs, his gaze bouncing between me and my mentor. "Fuck you."

Clearly not the demon's name. Even if appropriate for a walking evil entity.

Why don't you use the spell for identifying the demon? I stare at the back of Smythe's head as he gives it a slight shake.

Don't want the others to know that spell.

I'm about to ask why not but keep the thought to myself. Smythe doesn't need the distraction of another conversation. And the more I think on it, the more I realize why not. The powerful spell comes from the depths of Hades. Why admit he knows a spell written by a demon? Furthermore, why give away an advantage?

"Who is your demon?" He asks again, this time lacing his words with a dose of compulsion.

The minion's lips twitch with an effort not to speak. Not even a FU escapes.

"Who is your demon?" This time the two other mages join in the questioning, all three sending compulsion along the words.

A full body shiver rolls through the minion.

"Mammon." The name escapes as a whisper.

Ah-ha! But why would the demon of greed shoot up the Emergency Department? Wouldn't he rather rob a bank?

"Why did Mammon send you to the hospital?" Smythe leans forward, resting his elbows on the table, for all appearances calm and collected. But I sense the excitement running through him, a live wire of energy.

The minion shakes his head in refusal. Only to be asked the same question by all three mages.

Tremors shake his limbs as he tries to resist. But the compulsion forces the truth despite his struggle. "To find and kill the *Justitian*."

"Why?"

The minion looks at the table, shaking his head. But he answers before the trio can ask. "We missed the last time. She needs to die." His focus snaps from the table to me.

Good thing my back is already against the wall since the force of his glare would knock me back a step. Hate glimmers in the depths of his black gaze. A hatred not normally sent my way. Minions fight me, want me dead, try to kill me, but it's all in a day's work. They don't normally throw that much hatred my direction.

Why? Why would this minion hate me that much?

Apparently I projected that thought to Smythe, who asks the question of the minion. Any other time the fact I projected a thought would bother me. But not today. Today I want to know the answer, want to know why I'm targeted by a demon for death.

"Why are you targeting the *Justitian*? What did she do to make Mammon want her dead so badly?"

White-knuckled fists clutch the chains shackling

him to the table. He pulls. The chains clink, rattling against the metal table, but hold. His lips twitch as he tries to fight the compulsion. His body jerks as the words explode from his lips in a rush. "She's disrupting his plans."

"What plans?"

He shakes his head. "I don't know more than that. All I know is he wants her dead. She's meddling in his life, his plans. That's all I know, man. All I know."

Smythe glances at the two mages. They both shrug. He rolls his fingers against the table as he stares at the minion.

"Where—"

Whatever he plans on saying fizzles on his lips as the door bangs open, Samantha striding inside like a Valkyrie bent on revenge. Her black T-shirt and jeans hug her athletic figure like a second skin. Combat boots beat the floor as she stalks to the table. I straighten, shoving off the wall while giving her my best glare. Not that she notices. Her gaze remains locked on Smythe. Looks like David lied when he said he'd punish her for hiring a regiment of minions to kill me. More proof Smythe's father didn't believe us.

Or is in cahoots with the ones who financed her misplaced loyalty.

I'm going with the latter. David's as guilty as Samantha. One of these days we'll discover the why of the matter.

"What are you doing?" Samantha's glare bounces between Smythe and the minion, who knocks his chair over and jumps back as far as his chains will allow.

As if he thinks the blonde, bitch mage will annihilate him on sight.

Smythe shoves his chair back, stands and faces her, arms crossed. "Questioning the minion. What are you doing?"

TaRhonda and Delores stand beside him, mirroring his posture. All for one and one for all, I guess.

Samantha doesn't spare them the trouble of a quick glance. As if she fails to notice the female mages glaring at her. Guess I'm not the only one having blonde bitch mage issues.

"You brought a minion to the Agency?"

"You know as well as I it's been done before when information is needed. Information was needed." His eyes narrow. "You know he's a minion or you wouldn't be here. What do you want? Besides interrupting my interrogation."

She glances at the pale-faced minion for a second. "Your father has questions."

"Tell him to come ask me himself."

"He said you needed to come to the briefing room."

"I'm in the middle of questioning. As you can see."

"Too bad. He sent me to get you. Now." She turns her head and stares at me, her upper lip twisting into a sneer. "And bring her too."

I open my mouth, shut it just as quick. No sense in antagonizing her already pissy self. At least not right now. An undercurrent of malevolence runs through the room, cold and slithering, brushing against my skin. Ice slides down my spine, a warning to keep my lips sealed and locked. A warning I obey.

Demon? Confusion laces the *justitia's* tone.

Could it mean Samantha is a demon? If so, wouldn't Zagan's counterspell show me she was the demon? Since I remain clueless as to the demon's identity, I assume the *justitia* picks up on Samantha's normal bitchy demeanor and confuses it for a demon.

No demon. Samantha's just a bitch. Unless you know she's the demon?

Yes. Bitch. Demon no. But close. She near demon.

Since she stands near Smythe and I know for a fact he's not the demon, I assume the *justitia* means she's been in close proximity of the demon. But just in case…

Do you sense a demon nearby?

Here has demon. Demon here but not seen. Hiding. You find. I kill. Master happy.

Geez, Louise. Not the whole make-Zagan-happy speech again. *He's not our master. He's a friend. And unless you sense a demon in the immediate vicinity, I need to pay attention to what's going on with Smythe and Samantha.*

The *justitia* huffs, retreating into itself. Which I take as a sign a demon isn't nearby.

I suppose it's a good thing Samantha is a garden variety bitch and not a bitch masquerading as a demon.

Smythe stares at the blonde mage for another tension-filled moment. He gestures toward the door.

"You first."

"What?" Sculpted brows rise.

"You first. Lead the way, Samantha."

Her eyes narrow, gaze darting to the cowering minion. After giving Smythe a squinty-eyed glare, she turns on her heel and marches out the door. Smythe tilts his head her direction and the two mages follow. He holds his hand out to me, a silent request to step in front of him.

Seriously? Samantha might not be the Agency demon, but according to my *justitia*, she's been near one. Who's to say following her isn't some sort of a set-up? I raise a what-the-hell brow at Smythe.

Who shakes his head. *Go on, I know what I'm doing. She's not leading us into a trap.*

Okay then. He might not think it a trap, but I'll continue to be on guard in case he's wrong.

Right as we're about to leave the room, the minion screeches.

"Don't leave me here! They'll kill me! Don't leave me!"

Pausing in the doorway, Smythe draws in a breath. "You were dead the moment you agreed to consort with a demon." Without turning, he pulls the door shut behind him, the snick of the lock sealing in the hollering minion.

What did the thing expect? Candy and flowers for a job well done? He had to have known when we brought him here we weren't planning on setting him free.

At the same time, while I knew the minion's ending, his fear of death struck me as odd. As Smythe said, the minion knew what he was signing up for when he agreed to raid the hospital and try to kill me, so why was he so scared when death looked him in the eyes?

Five sets of thudding footsteps echo along the dim hallway. The minion's screams fade as we stride closer toward the elevator. Samantha hits the button like she holds a grudge against the thing, and with a loud ding the doors oblige her impatience by opening without a wait.

Great. Part of me wanted a pause on the action, an extremely long pause before having to speak with

David. Simply being in the same room with the man riles my temper. Besides, the minion's cocky attitude turning into one of intimidation and fear is concerning.

While I can't do a damn thing about David's attitude, I can ask about the minion's odd behavior. Telepathy to the rescue.

As we walk into the elevator, I cut Smythe a sideways glance, catching his attention. Then I stick mental barriers in place and hope they hold against prying mages.

Which should work. Samantha tried to kill me, but she's never tried to read my mind. I doubt TaRhonda and Delores want to take a journey through my thoughts and I'm speaking with the biggest prying mage at the Agency.

No problem.

Why was that minion so scared to be left alone? He knew he was going to die.

A small wrinkle forms between Smythe's brows. *I don't know. They aren't normally afraid of death. Something about the demonic essence makes them lack fear.*

Maybe it wore off? Or he had second thoughts about dying?

Nope. It doesn't wear off. No second thoughts for minions.

Which brings me to another minion topic. *How do you kill them after questioning?*

The impression he rolls his eyes drifts into my mind, although he remains staring at the metal doors as if lost in his own thoughts and not our conversation. *The only way possible. With a* justitia.

So they aren't tortured?

Not normally, no. It's a clean kill. And it hurts the demon.

Then he shouldn't have been hollering.

No. He shouldn't.

You think he's afraid Mammon will kill him? In a way worse than a Justitian?

We step out of the elevator into the typical Agency opulent hallway. The door slides shut behind us as we follow Samantha to the briefing room. Smythe continues our conversation as we walk.

That would confirm Mammon is the Agency demon.

You already suspected him. He's the only name on a list of possibilities. It makes sense.

It would explain the minion's fear. He talked. His master will know and kill him. He stops walking, his face a mask of oh-shit. *Fuck. Samantha wasn't leading us into a trap. She was leading us away from one. The minion wasn't trying to play our emotions, he was speaking the truth. We need to get back there before Mammon does, so we know whose face the demon hides behind.*

He grabs my arm and hauls me toward the elevator. No complaints from me. Discovering the identity of the demon is high priority.

And as a bonus, I don't have to see David.

"Hey!" Samantha shouts to our retreating backsides.

But like a dog who comes when called, the elevator opens with a push of the button and a ding, ushering us inside. Smythe shoves the down button and the door closes on a pissed off, yelling Samantha.

"Do you—" my gaze snags on my sword before I can finish the sentence.

The *justitia* remains a sword.

What the hell? It should've changed into a bracelet after we left the interrogation room.

I hold my wrist up. "Why is this still a sword?"

And what does it say about me that it's taken me until now to notice it's still a freaking sword?

A thought I refuse to voice. Some answers aren't worth knowing.

"Because of the minion?"

"Too far away." I shake my head. This has to be the longest time the thing has remained in sword form without being in the presence of a demonic entity.

"But growing closer by the second."

"Come on, Smythe. Why's it still a sword?"

"You've said it yourself. It always reacts oddly around the Agency. The demon's presence confuses it. And we're heading back toward the minion."

"It remained a sword walking toward the briefing room."

He gives me a brow-raised pause. "Is it telling you there's a demon?"

"No." *Are you?*

The elevator slides to a stop at the basement, doors opening on cool air. The entity's purple essence explodes along my nerves, a shout of glee.

Demon! Kill demon!

I raise my eyes to meet Smythe's. "I was wrong. It's now saying there's a demon."

"Then why are we standing around?"

Good question.

We dash down the hall toward the interrogation room. Even from a distance I can tell the door hangs open as if a large, super-mad creature tore it half off its hinges. The closer we get, the stronger the metallic scent of blood. We stop at the broken door.

No need to go inside. There's enough blood spatter to declare the minion dead without bothering with a pulse. The fact his head and hands—was that his tongue across the room? Eww—were separated from his body also helped. I swallow as stomach acid bubbles into my throat.

Yeah, I kill minions. But I don't torture them.

I clasp a hand over my mouth, trying to keep my stomach contents in their correct place.

"Damn it!" Smythe stalks around the room, avoiding the crimson pools of blood. "We weren't quick enough."

I swallow, once, twice, before convinced my lunch won't make a reappearance. "He hasn't been dead long. The blood's not clotted."

"Do you sense the demon?"

I close my eyes. Not that I need to do so to talk to the *justitia*, but the action makes me look like I'm trying to solve his question.

Where's the demon?

Close.

A faint ding breaks my concentration. I open my eyes to a curious Smythe, who speaks before me.

"What did it say?"

"The demon is close."

"Where?"

Once again I close my eyes. *Can we track him?*

Coming to you. Greedy, greedy, greedy.

This time I speak while opening my eyes. "It says the demon is coming to us."

His lips twitch like he's about to say something,

but then he stiffens, his gaze darting behind me, to the hanging door. His eyes narrow.

"Samantha."

No wonder he stares at the doorway. Samantha, my "favorite" mage, stands with her hands on her slim hips, her glare turning pretty features into hateful rage.

"I heard what she said. You think I had something to do with this?" She gestures toward the downed minion.

Light catches the silver of my sword as I shift my position. The *justitia* said the demon was coming my way. Maybe Samantha is the demon? As much as I'd like her to be, earlier my *justitia* said she was a bitch not a demon.

Sitting around waiting for a demon to appear so I can off it is not my normal routine. Getting out of my routine makes me edgy.

Or maybe that's because this no-good blonde glares at me.

"Why not?" I return her glare. "You tried to kill me several months back. Who's to say you aren't working for a demon?"

Red colors her cheeks as her eyes narrow. "How dare you? I am a mage."

"A lying—"

Smythe grabs my arm, forcing me to shut my mouth. "Do you know what happened, Samantha?"

Her glare stings as she focuses on him. "Isn't it obvious? The minion was killed. An unauthorized kill, by the looks of it. How can you let her accuse me of this?"

Smythe raises a brow at her fake whine and stares at her for several heartbeats, until her face turns the purple-red color of a person two seconds away from exploding a stream of obscenities.

She's guilty. If my *justitia* thinks she smells like a demon, then she's been hanging out with one. While I'd like to give her the benefit of the doubt, to believe her rubbing elbows with a demon was accidental, the truth is she hired minions to kill me. You can't wipe that fact away. She smells like a demon not due to some accidental touch while walking down the hall, but because she works for the beast.

I knew she was rotten from the get-go.

Heavy footsteps echo on the linoleum, drawing closer with each beat, interrupting my thoughts and the stare-and-glare between Samantha and Smythe. Who's coming our way? Definitely not TaRhonda or Delores. The footsteps indicate bigger bodies than theirs. Besides, I doubt either of them want to return to this room.

A prickling sensation fires along my nerves, as excitement bubbles through my veins. Both courtesy of the *justitia*.

And we all know what that means. As the witches in Macbeth said, something wicked this way comes.

Check me out. I really did learn something in high school English.

"This isn't over." Samantha hisses, as she turns to face the newcomers.

Charles Tweedy and David stop outside the room.

Demon. The eerie voice of my *justitia* slams into my mind.

Well, well, well, why am I not surprised the thing thinks one of them is the demon? But which one?

Puzzlement shivers along my nerves as the entity

tries to determine which man is demonic. I activate the minion and demon sensors in my eyes, but all I see is a glob of red-orange tinged in black.

On both men. Not a lot of help there. And while I lean toward David being the badass, what if I'm wrong? I'm not making another mistake by killing a human.

I'm jarred back to the present by the squeak of the broken door as the men walk into the room. The trails fade as I turn off the sensors to focus on the more important action.

"What's going on here?" David glares at his son. "We heard you captured a minion for interrogation." His gaze bounces to the blood-spattered room. Instead of shock or stopping a gag reflex, he acts like a headless, handless, tongueless minion is par for the course.

So does Chuck. No change, no surprise, no emotion.

It's not like they came in after a minion-*Justitian* fight. This was outright slaughter. They should feel something.

Demon. Confidence laces the *justitia's* tone, its earlier puzzlement vanishing under an air of awareness. A shiver jostles the silver links against my wrist, shaking a hidden memory free.

I draw in a breath as memories swirl through my mind. Memories of T telling me the identity of the Agency demon. Again and again and again. Even though we all forgot the name every time he said it. Other memories join in, small clues put together forming an answer I knew and forgot.

But no longer. His name slams into my mind. The knowledge fills my *justitia* with a murderous rage and it's all I can do to stop the thing from stabbing him in the heart. We need to know who else its evil has infected, know how far its influence reaches, before I kill him.

Smythe stiffens, his grip on my arm tightening as his eyes widen. I try to hop into his mind only to ram against a foot-thick barrier. Doesn't matter. I know what he's thinking. He remembers the same thing I do.

The identity of the demon.

My gaze snags on the two men as I try my damndest to wipe my face free from shock. The demon isn't who I thought it was. It's worse. Instead of Smythe's father David, the demon is the leader of the Agency.

Chuck Tweedy.

Chapter Eighteen

Chuck glances at me, his gaze focusing on my *justitia*. His brows pull together. Oh shit. I throw up all the mental barriers I possess and hope they work against a demon trying to read my mind to discover why the *justitia* remains a sword.

But despite a slight smile tugging the corners of his lips, he maintains a mask of indifference. Just like David. Only not as blustery.

Typical David behavior. Geez Louise, but the man's a gigantic turd. Fortunately for Smythe, he's not a demon.

Surprise, surprise, surprise.

I still vote David's in cahoots with one. And not in the 'my boss is a demon' type of way either.

Don't kill Chuck! Smythe yells telepathically. *We don't know the extent of his deception.*

Which corresponds to my line of thinking on the matter. This is one demon I can't annihilate on contact. What if the entire Agency is on his side? For starters, we wouldn't make it out of here alive. A trade I'd be willing to make if it guaran-damn-teed the demon and anyone following him died.

A guarantee impossible to make.

Got it. Agreed.

My *justitia* rattles its links around my wrist, irritation spiking along my nerves. *Demon!*

Quiet! Wait.

It settles with a huff, a calmness I know won't last for long.

"I said," David takes a step toward his son, appearing unaware of our sudden demon knowledge, "what's going on in here? Why's the minion dead? You can't question a dead minion."

"They're accusing me of killing him even though we were all heading toward the briefing room when it happened." Samantha gives me another glare, crosses her arms over her chest and does her best impression of a whining toddler.

Lips pressed into a frown, Smythe releases an audible breath of air through his nose. He's as annoyed at Samantha as I am. Maybe more so.

Nah. No way could he be more annoyed at the blonde mage. She didn't hire minions to kill him. He's nothing more than garden variety annoyed, unlike me who continues to hold on to a grudge as if it's a lifesaver.

Smythe gives my arm a small, quick squeeze, the nonverbal equivalent of hush-it. I decide he has a point, press my lips together, and wrap my irritation, anger, and surprise around me like a cloak.

Ignoring Samantha, he addresses his father. "We were heading to the briefing room to meet you when Gin and I realized something was wrong with the minion."

"How?" David crosses his arms. "What made you come back?"

Smythe shrugs. "A feeling. And we were right. We left the minion alive for another round of questioning."

"Who'd kill him so viciously?" David gestures to

the dead body, as if he didn't already know the answer: his uber-muscled boss. "A mess is what it is. And the demon's essence went back to the demon. Did you even bother to lock the door?"

Smythe crosses his arms, eyes narrowing, as he draws in another noisy breath through his nose. "The doors automatically lock when the door is closed. You know this. Do you really think the minion would've let in his killer? You know as well as I it has to be someone at the Agency. One of us."

David presses his lips together until white lines form at the corners of his mouth.

"Perhaps we should review the video." Chuck gestures to a camera in the interrogation room.

Right. Because mages have no problem scrubbing security footage to get away with a little B&E. Or minion killing, as the case may be.

Kill demon, kill demon, kill demon. The *justitia* chants in my head, the refrain punctuated by small movements of my arm making me look like a drunken puppet.

I clasp my left hand on my right wrist. The pose appears calm, but in reality it keeps my *justitia* from forcing my arm to whack off Chuck's head. Despite the thing's inclination to rid the world of another demon, we need to know how deep Chuck's takeover goes. Like Smythe said, we shouldn't kill him until we know who else is involved, until we know if he has help.

Duh. Of course he has help. Like the blonde mage standing across from me. Samantha used funds dumped into her account to hire minions to kill me. Funds sent from the Agency. Clearly she's not the bright and flawless mage she calls herself.

The gotcha grin crossing Smythe's face snaps me back to the present. What did I miss by tripping through my thoughts?

Apparently nothing, as Smythe responds to Chuck's comment.

"Good idea. Ask security about the footage. Since it can't be obscured, we should be able to tell who killed him."

What do you mean, it can't be obscured? I drop my mental barriers a tad to talk to Smythe. *You change them all the time when needed.*

Not the ones at the Agency. These have a spell to render them impervious to magical tampering. Now be quiet.

Huh. You learn something new every day. Despite Smythe's assurance, a niggling internal voice questions if his confidence in spells is misplaced. What if Chuck the demon has a spell to change the video feed? After all, he possessed a powerful forget-me spell unable to be reversed without the help of another demon.

David pulls his phone out of his pocket, pushes numbers on the screen, and places it against his ear. "Pull the security footage from interrogation room five. Send it to the briefing room. We'll be there in a couple of minutes to review." He ends the call and places the phone back into his pocket.

"Let's go." Without glancing at the minion, David turns and marches out the door.

I want to ask who's going to clean up the mess, but the question isn't as important as what's about to happen, so I keep my mouth shut. Twice in under ten minutes. Must be a record.

The elevator dings an arrival notice, its buzz

echoing down the hall. We pile inside, silent except for hushed breathing.

Demon! Kill demon! My *justitia* shrieks inside my head.

Dammit. I knew the thing wouldn't stay quiet. Or listen to Smythe's reasoning. But I give explaining another shot as I struggle to keep my arm by my side. *I can't! We don't know how far his deception goes.*

Lie. I see. I know. Kill demon.

I will. But not now. He's cast a spell on everyone to hide his true self. If I kill him now, they'll kill me.

Kill demon.

Not convinced of my attempt to explain, the thing struggles to make me stab Chuck in the back.

Calm down! Stop that! I grab my wrist, pulling my arm to my leg, while the entity struggles to force me to perform a slice-and-dice move. *Turn into the bracelet.*

No! Kill demon.

Chuck will die. I promise. Just not now. Turn into the bracelet. Or you'll give us away.

My body vibrates as the entity along my nerves hums in disgust. For a long moment I think it's going make another stab-through-the-heart attempt. But with a final shake of disgust, it turns into the silver linked bracelet right as the elevator doors slide open.

Better kill demon soon. Not happy to wait.

Yeah, yeah, yeah. I get it. We'll get him. Soon.

I hope.

Smythe places a hand on my shoulder as we follow David and Samantha down the hall, Chuck trailing us like a guard. Now that I know who the demon is, how could I not have sensed him before, even with the forget-me spell? His presence thickens the air with the stench of sulfur.

I activate the demon/minion receptors in my eyes and stifle a gasp. Red-orange demon trails overlaid with a thick black cloud coat the gilded hallways like a spreading malignancy. Cold brushes against my spine, a skeletal finger of death. Evil stalks me, trying to worm its way under my skin, trying to gain control. I sense it as surely as T senses ghosts.

How many people has he infected? Samantha? David? Do they know they work for a demon and not care? Or are they clueless, a victim of the forget-me spell? Are we the only ones who know what he is?

My gaze focuses on David and Samantha, on their straight spines and over-confident strides. Red-orange and black demonic essence covers their bodies, a suffocating blanket of malevolence.

I'm betting they know exactly who they work for and have no problems with selling their souls for a measly reward. But what reward? And how many others are complacent to the evil among us?

I suck in a short gasp of air as my stomach becomes heavy. Why did I not notice the evident demonic infection spread across their bodies before now? How could I have missed it? My only excuse is I never bothered to use my minion/demon sensors inside the Agency until today.

Poor excuse. I should have noticed. Forget-me spell be damned.

David opens the door to the briefing room and gestures us inside, the motion snapping me back to the present. TaRhonda and Delores are already seated in chairs around a long conference table. Do they have anything to do with the demon? Do they know what happened to the demon? Or are they good little mages, oblivious to the demon, believing the Agency and all its workers are exactly who they pretend?

I stare at them, looking for, and finding, their upper body surrounded by the demonic essence. Although it's not as thick as what surrounds David and Samantha. Does that mean they aren't as high up in the demon hierarchy? Have they only had casual contact with Chuck? Or are they as guilty as David and Samantha?

I turn to Smythe. Like the female mages, vague traces of demonic essence surround his upper body. Very light and hard to see, yet nonetheless present. Since he's not in bed with the demon, I assume the light demon traces around him and the two female mages mean casual contact with Chuck.

But what if I'm wrong? About the female mages, that is.

Smythe! Look at the demon trails!

Close your mind, Gin! We'll discuss it later. Smythe's hand on my shoulder tightens in a subtle warning.

Shit. Did I project my thoughts to someone beside Smythe? Who else heard me? I throw all the mental barriers I possess around my thoughts, locking them down, hiding them from prying minds.

Smythe leads me to a chair next to the two mages and takes the one next to me. Samantha and Chuck sit across from us. David fiddles with the projector until the interrogation room appears on the screen.

The camera sits above the door so we get a direct shot of the yelling minion. His body strains against his shackles as his lips form silent words. Unfortunately the camera doesn't pick up sound, but the words his lips form are clear. *Don't leave me here! He'll kill me!*

He yanks on his chains as if expecting the links to mysteriously unlock. Giving up, he sits for about a minute, his fingers twisting against the cuffs on his wrist. Then his head pops up, his gaze focusing on the door. His eyes widen as he shoves back the chair, as he tries to move away from the table. The shackles snap him to a stop, hindering his escape. He shakes his head, pleading to whoever stands in the doorway for forgiveness.

And that's when things get weird. First, his tongue flies out of his mouth, carved out by an unseen hand. I jump, clasping a palm across my lips, and swallow. Hard.

The minion's body is thrown across the room, minus his hands, which remain shackled to the table as bloody stumps. A blur whirls toward the wailing minion. When it disappears, the minion's body and head lay separated on the floor.

I swallow, willing my stomach contents to remain where they belong. I kill minions all the time with no physical effect, but this killing makes me sick. Probably because the minions I fight aren't terrorized.

Smythe taps the table to catch David's attention. "Replay the blur on slow-motion."

David pushes a couple of buttons and the video replays from when the blur enters the room. The video moves forward one frame at a time. In theory, the blur should disappear, leaving behind frame-shots of who attacked the minion.

I am one hundred percent certain the killer sits in this room, but confirmation would be nice.

Unfortunately, the blur remains a blur, even at a

frame by frame pace.

Damn it. I really wanted to see Chuck or David's face on the screen.

"That doesn't tell us anything." Samantha stares at David after cutting me a glare.

Smythe shakes his head, answering before his father. "On the contrary, it tells us a lot. Whoever killed the minion possesses the ability to either change the spell on the security footage or is powerful enough to move faster than the camera lens can capture. Who among us can perform that magic? Not me."

David reddens, glaring at his son as if Smythe referred to him. Good guess. Maybe he did. If not, Smythe should have. As much as I'd love to blame the minion's death on Samantha, I know she didn't do it. David could have, though, easily. So could Chuck, our resident demon.

Does David know Chuck is a demon? Is David working for him, or does his shadiness come about naturally?

All thoughts for another time. Like when we get out of here. Provided we get out of here alive.

"My son's right. It tells us a lot. But not who the killer is. No mage would kill a minion held for interrogation. I'm not sure any of our mages are powerful enough to pull off that blur," David gestures toward the screen. "Not even Samantha."

She glares, clearly not happy about being labeled not so powerful.

David turns to the two mages sitting beside me. "Did either of you notice anything strange in the interrogation room?"

"No, sir." They answer simultaneously.

"All right. You're dismissed. If you think of anything else, let me know."

They nod at him as they walk out the door. David leans back in his chair, his eyes narrowing on Smythe.

"Son, I don't know what went on in there"—again, he gestures at the still frame of the dead minion—"but Samantha didn't have anything to do with it."

Right. Of course not. While I know she didn't personally kill the minion—unless she's upgraded to a whole new set of skills—she knew him. He wouldn't have been so afraid of her otherwise.

But pointing it out would not be in my best interest. At least not at the moment.

Three times in a day I've kept my mouth shut. I'm going for the gold.

"Who do you think did?" Keeping his gaze on David, Smythe manages to look curious instead of side-eyeing Chuck like I would've done.

David shakes his head, continuing to stare at the screen as if it holds answers. I've got to admit: the man appears convincing. Unfortunately for him, I'm not convinced. Fortunately for me, I can act like I am.

"Don't know." David drums his fingers against the table, his brows pulling together, giving the appearance he's thinking of a guilty party.

Or a convincing lie to throw suspicion off the true perpetrator.

"Chuck?" David punts to the demon.

Grabbing my bracelet-covered wrist on the off-chance the *justitia* once again tries to take control of my arm, I face Chuck while schooling my face into what I hope is a look of curiosity.

The demon stares a bit too long at Smythe's dad

before sighing. "You're right, our mages aren't powerful enough to counteract the spell on the security camera. Nor can they move fast enough to fool the camera lens, as your son pointed out. As much as it pains me to say this, it appears we've been infiltrated by a demon. But how? And which one?"

Shock widens my eyes. Appropriate for the situation and not at all faked. Out of all the answers Chuck could have given, pointing out a demon in the Agency—a step away from admitting he killed the minion—was not what I expected.

"Don't be ridiculous," Smythe inserts, once again a response I wasn't expecting. "If a demon was present, don't you think Gin's *justitia* would've turned into a sword? It's only been a sword around the minion. There has to be another explanation."

The corners of Chuck's lips turn into a grin. "There is no other explanation. A demon has infiltrated our Agency." The smile drops from his lips as he releases a sigh coupled with a head shake. "Unfortunately, I have an idea of who it is."

He pauses for dramatic effect. Oh boy, this should be interesting. Once he has our full attention, he speaks the one name guaran-damn-teed to change everything.

"The healer, Eloise."

Chapter Nineteen

My eyes pop so wide they hurt, the expression not faked. Oh shit. He somehow knows Eloise is after him and has decided to turn the tables. Does he realize Smythe and I are on to him, too? Is this a ruse to get us to kill Eloise under false pretenses?

I'm too dumbfounded to speak.

Luckily, Smythe recovers after a blink and a head shake. "Can't be. She's helped heal Gin too many times."

Chuck shrugs. "How better to hide in plain sight than to blend in, pretend to be helpful."

I swallow, intending to defend my friend, but David talks first.

"You know, that makes sense. I've heard rumors she came to the Agency from Hell. She could easily not be who she says she is."

"But—"

Smythe tramples right over my attempted defense. "I haven't heard that rumor, Dad. If so, then you have a point. She could very well be someone else."

I try not to sigh in relief. For a brief second, when he first interrupted me, I feared Smythe was agreeing with them. I should've known better. He wouldn't agree with them. His words are a warning for me to shut the fuck up and let him handle the situation.

Since my outspoken mouth has been—

occasionally—known to get me in trouble, I heed his underlying communication. Although I do shake my head, because I need to do something besides sit there. They know Eloise is my friend, at least I assume they do. I should act shocked and try to defend her.

Unless Smythe offers a good explanation for how she could have deceived us.

Smythe pats my arm, turns to face me. "I know this is hard after all the times she's healed you, but you've got to admit they have a point. Why else would she have come to the Agency from Hell?"

Despite knowing the correct answer—family issues can be a bitch—I force a pensive expression on my face. Give a swallow and a big sigh and nod. "I suppose you have a point."

David raises a brow as if surprised I can see reason. Let's hope it's not a big enough surprise to get him thinking I'm lying.

I'm not really lying. Smythe does have a point. The point being I need to play along with him in order to get out of this situation and warn Eloise.

"Good. Because I think we"—he gestures between the two of us—"need to hunt her down and bring her in for questioning."

David's eyes narrow. "Are you sure, son? You've been close with her."

"A little too close," Samantha adds.

Smythe glares at them both. "If she's a demon, it doesn't matter how close we've been. Besides, she didn't come when Mom needed her. If she had, the outcome would have been different. Let's just say after all these years, I still hold a grudge." His jaw tenses.

His act is totally believable. Actually, I'll bet

money it isn't an act. After his mom drank herself into a coma and Eloise didn't come to heal her after repeat requests, he probably does hold a grudge. Knowing Smythe, though, it's not a huge one. His mom remains in a coma, even after all these years. He and David had to learn how to get along without her in their lives.

I know how it affected Smythe, but what about David? How much does he miss his wife? Has he learned to live without her, or does he still long to talk to her? Or was their relationship so bad he doesn't give a shit she's in a vegetative state?

All thoughts for another day. Provided I live to see that day.

David nods, his expression relaxing as he buys Smythe's story. "So do I, son, so do I." He draws in a breath as if trying to erase unhappy memories. "Okay"—his gaze darts to Chuck for a moment—"you and Gin can hunt her down. Take her alive. We need to question her. To see how far her influence reaches."

Smythe shoves his chair back and stands. "You won't be disappointed." He grips my shoulder a bit too hard. "Come on, Gin. Let's get going."

As I stand, his hand drops and I walk to the door while he speaks to the others.

"We'll start with a sweep of the Agency. See if we can pick up on her presence."

"Start with the infirmary," Chuck says like we're a bunch of dummies.

But I give him the obligatory nod as if he had the best idea in the world. His self-satisfied smile indicates he believes we've fallen for his lies.

At least I hope that's what it means. Drawing in a deep breath, I open the door and step into the hall. No one greets me with a weapon and I release my held breath in a whoosh of air.

Smythe strides past me, heading for the elevator.

Can they hear telepathic thoughts? I know better than to speak aloud. He once told me the Agency walls possess magical ears. I don't remember asking if the spells read thoughts.

Not unless they are close by or we project a thought to them. They don't coat the walls with spells to listen in telepathically.

Good. So we can talk?

Not here.

He steps in front of the elevator and pushes the up button. This time we wait a minute until it arrives with a loud *ding.* We step inside, he pushes the floor for the infirmary, and stands with his arms crossed, staring at the closed doors.

Now we can talk. But stare straight ahead. The elevators have cameras.

I mirror his pose. *I can't believe he accused Eloise.*

I can. What better way to throw the scent off himself than accusing someone else? He confirmed what she told us, she came to the Agency after a stint in Hell.

You do still believe her, right?

He stiffens. *Of course. How can you think otherwise?*

I don't. We know Chuck's the demon. Not only did we realize it when we saw him today, but my justitia *confirmed it. I don't want to believe it, but what if Eloise played us like Chuck did? What if she's working with Zagan to take control of Hell?*

Good lord, Gin. Stop being such a conspiracy

theorist. She's a nephilim. Other angels consider nephilim to be an abomination so it's not hard to believe they threw her out of Heaven and she took a trip to Hell to piss them off, learned her mistake, and tried to atone for it. She's been at the Agency for a century and during that time has done nothing but heal others and help when needed.

Except for your mom.

The elevator dings an arrival notice to the infirmary. Smythe shoots me a glare as he steps into the not-so-busy healers' domain.

That was low.

You didn't fake the still holding a grudge thing.

I want Mom back to how I remember her, that's true. But how I want her to be and how she truly was are two different things. She loved me, but she was sad all the time. Is it right to bring her back when she was clearly suffering? I don't think so. She's better off where she is. So, no. I don't hold a grudge. Eloise can't be expected to be in all places at all times.

He pauses. *How did you know about Mom?*

Oops. Eloise made me promise not to ask Smythe about his mother after she told me the woman drank herself into a vegetative state. So much for my promise.

A little birdy. I'm sorry about your mom.

For a moment, he looks like he's going to ask me the little birdy's identity. He finally sighs. *I should have told you earlier.*

No harm done. I'm glad you don't hold a grudge against Eloise. Or guessed she's the little birdy.

We walk up and down the hall, peering into each curtain-surrounded exam room as if we actually expect Eloise to be here instead of either in her quarters or the library with T. Our conversation continues as we walk.

Dad feels differently. He's never forgiven Eloise for letting Mom slip into a coma. Like she poured drinks down Mom's throat. He gives a quick head shake as he peers into another exam room.

What are we going to do? How are we going to get Eloise out of here?

I've been trying to call her, but all her barriers are up. She's either in her room or the library with your brother.

That's exactly what I thought. Should we head there?

No. If we make a direct beeline to her they might suspect something.

Or maybe they'll suspect something if we continue to walk around the infirmary even though it's obvious she's not here. Maybe we should go to where we think she'll be. After all, they know we're friends.

He rubs the back of his neck. *We're damned if we do and damned if we don't.*

Kill demon, my *justitia* chimes in, *then no be damned.*

My justitia *is saying to kill the demon. Which has pretty much been its chant since Chuck walked into the interrogation room.*

Smythe stops, a puzzled expression on his face. *Why didn't it know who Chuck was before now?*

Me only suspect. If you under spell, me under spell. Me feel demon here but not know who. Demon cast strong spell.

I repeat its words to Smythe. He nods.

Okay. Makes sense. His eyes widen as a small smile curves his lips. *Try calling T.*

What a moron. I should've thought to call my brother. Sometimes I wonder about myself.

T! I project my words to my twin. *It's an emergency!*

A rush of anger fills my being as he steps into my mind.

What's wrong? What is it?

The demon's Chuck—

Shit! I remember now. He's the—

I know. That's not the emergency. Chuck has accused Eloise of being a demon and we've been sent to hunt her down and bring her in for questioning.

What the fuck?

Yeah, yeah, I'm there with you, but we need to know where you all are so you can get out of here.

We're in the library but we're leaving. I'll let you know where we land.

Good. Get out of here now. We're not sure if they're following us to get to you or have sent us to the infirmary so they can arrest her. Run!

We're gone. He shuts off our communication, leaving behind a swirl of anger.

I grab Smythe's arm. *Got him and he said they're leaving. He'll contact me when they find a safe place.*

Good. Let's go walk through the building like we did earlier. This time we can see the demon essence.

Not sure if it'll help. You have demon essence around your upper body.

What! Wide eyes reflect his horror.

I don't blame him. I'd freak too if someone told me I was surrounded by a demonic essence.

No joke. So did the two female mages, but none of you have the trails as dark as your father and

Samantha.

Smythe shoves the down button on the elevator. "Let's check out the landing room. We'll see if she came in or out of there recently and pick up video surveillance of the building."

"Sounds good." My voice sounds a little off to my ears since I'm thrown by the conversation change.

Although I understand the need to talk so the cameras show us behaving normally, it throws me off a bit. And I'm freakin' nervous about blowing the spy shit and giving away Eloise's location. Or our knowledge.

I'm better at slicing and dicing and tracking minions than undercover agent.

A tone of irritation laces Smythe's voice in my head. *I saw the same trails you did around the others, but never realized the trails covered me too. You're saying I look like I've been touched by a demon?*

Yep. Sorry. Do they cover me?

No.

Maybe it's from casual contact with Chuck. I can't believe neither of us thought to look for demon trails in the Agency.

Sounds like the forget-me spell also caused us not to think logically about finding the demon.

I shrug. Excuses might make us feel better, but they don't forgive us for our lapse of intelligence. *We can discuss later. Are we really going to get the surveillance video?*

His lips press together as if he wants to continue the presence of demonic trails conversation. With a grunt he drops the topic, focusing on my question. *What better way to determine if they've left the building?*

T said—

I know, and what if they were nabbed before leaving?

Good point.

What feels like writhing snakes fills my stomach at the thought of T not making it out of the building. I draw in deep breaths in an attempt to calm my rising panic.

Silence shrouds us during the ride. Once the elevator opens, we hightail it to the landing room. A few minutes later we walk out with a promise for the security footage to be sent to the computer in Smythe's apartment. My heart pounds an uneven rhythm as we head to his place. Were Eloise and T able to escape? Did Chuck suspect us of lying? Were we being watched?

The journey to the privacy of Smythe's apartment takes forever. I swear eyes watch our every step.

Chapter Twenty

Once we get to Smythe's apartment, he shuts the door behind us, and strides toward his office.

"Are you sure no one is watching us?"

Without stopping, he speaks over his shoulder. "Not in here they aren't. Come on. We need to find Eloise and T."

All-righty then. I follow him into his office where he sits at the desk and pulls up the requested security footage.

I look over his shoulder as he scrolls through different angles until he gets to the library. Multiple camera shots show the library is free and clear of Eloise and T. We look at different camera views throughout the building without a sign of the two. From all appearances, T and Eloise escaped.

Thank god.

Some of the tension tightening my muscles into knots releases.

Smythe rotates his chair to face me. "Where do you think they'd go?"

"No idea. T lives, lived, with me, so that's a no go. And even if the house hadn't burned down, it wouldn't be safe. Where do you think Eloise would go?"

He shakes his head. "No idea."

"Okay. So we have to wait until T calls us. He's blocking me. I've tried." More times than I want to mention. Nothing comes through our bond, not fear or safety. I can only assume and hope T is okay. "Should we look busy? Should we report to David our lack of findings?"

"We should. The problem is what does he know? I saw the same demon trails you did surround him, Chuck, and Samantha as well as the mages." He scrubs a hand down his face. "I don't want him to be bad."

I rub his arm. "I know." Unfortunately, he is, so what are we going to do about it?

A question I keep to myself. No need to rub in his father's demonic involvement. Smythe has eyes and can see for himself David's deception.

We need to focus on the immediate problem. Ensuring Eloise escaped. The security footage indicates they left, but we need to physically check her apartment since apartments don't contain cameras. Besides, Chuck and crew would expect us to pay her apartment a visit.

"Let's check out Eloise's apartment. I'm assuming they'll be watching to make sure we go there. Right?"

He nods, running a hand through his hair. "Yeah. Let's go."

One elevator ride later and we step off on the floor to her apartment. Only to see David leaning against the wall next to her door.

Crap.

"Dad." Whatever Smythe says next fades into nothing as a wave of pain and anger slams into my mind.

I stumble, catching myself with a hand against the wall as T's voice explodes in my mind.

Gin! Watch out! They grabbed us before we could leave and are holding us in a room that looks like a cop interrogation room.

Shit! Are you okay? Panic ricochets through my system. Through our bond I can see him in a room similar to the one the currently dead minion occupied.

So far. I haven't talked. Eloise is in the next room. Couldn't get through to you until now. They cast some spell to knock us out.

Thank god he was okay. How am I going to get him out? I'll find a way. He's my twin. I'd walk across hot coals barefooted for him. *We'll be there as soon as we can.*

A cold wave of hatred spreads as an undercurrent on a low growl. *The damn demon is in the room with Eloise and I can't do anything about it.*

Double shit. So not good on too many levels. We need to get her out. Now. To hell with how many people are influenced by the demon. Chuck needs to die. *We're—*

My words trail into nothing as I get a glimpse of David and Smythe posturing like they're about to come to blows. Their fingers flex and release as they glare at the other, the space between them thickening with power.

What the hell happened while I talked to T?

Gotta go. We have trouble. We'll be there as soon as we can.

T snaps closed the telepathic path as I stride toward the study in anger management.

"Hey, what's going on?"

"Stay out of it, Gin." Tension laces Smythe's words, no doubt due to his locked jaw.

David doesn't bother to answer. His response is to shove a hand my direction. A wave of air smacks into my chest and I stumble back a foot. Smythe throws out a hand and uses his magic to ensure I stay upright. Double shit, shite, and horse manure. Instead of a typical stare-and-glare game, this appears to be the mage version of a pissing contest.

What should I do? I need to tell Smythe where T and Eloise are, but doing so might interrupt his concentration. And judging by his tense jaw and a bead of sweat trickling down his cheek, he needs all the concentration he can get.

On the other hand, David looks equally bad, maybe worse, since two sweat lines make trails down his face.

Should I help T escape and leave the Smythes to a battle of wills? My inclination is to run to my twin and together we can free Eloise. But what if the bad guy expects me to come? What if a bunch of mages-turned-demon-helpers line the basement hallway waiting to kill me? What good would I be to T or Eloise then?

Not to mention plotting and strategizing aren't my strengths. Those qualities belong to my guardian mage. Who is currently in the middle of proving his magical strength to his father.

What should I do?

David takes a step to the side and the tension between him and his son ramps down a level. Smythe leans forward, eyes narrow, his muscles a tight coil.

"How could you, Dad? You let evil control you."

David crosses his arms, red highlighting his cheeks. "I did what I needed to do to help your mom."

"Help her?" Smythe straightens as if slapped. "She can't be healed. She'll stay in that nursing home until she dies."

"Do you have any idea how much that upscale

home costs? And they've helped her. She recognizes me."

"She can't recognize you, Dad. She's a vegetable. You're imagining it."

David snarls. "I am not. If you refuse to believe the truth, then that's your problem, son. I did what I needed to do in order to ensure her comfort. And Chuck promised he'd heal her once I got back Gin's *justitia*."

Ignoring Smythe's earlier command, I step toward the men. "What do you mean, you tried to take back my *justitia*? You gave Samantha money to hire minions to kill me?"

David's glare hits with almost as much force as his earlier wind gust, but this time I remain upright of my own volition. "Don't be ridiculous. Chuck sent the payment to her and she was more than willing to help. I refused to have a part in it. I knew my son would trace the payment. No, I worked in other ways, setting you up to be taken down, but you always prevailed." Disbelief punctuates his words. "Always. No matter who I planned for you to fight. Even after we tried to burn you out of your house."

Anger curls in my stomach. "You did that?"

"I could have died!" Smythe snarls.

David throws up his hands, in a hold-on motion. "I didn't realize you were over there. If I'd known, I would've insisted on a different time. I want you alive. I did all this for you."

Smythe blinks, shock spreading across his face until it morphs into a cold rage. His voice flattens into resolve. "You shouldn't have bothered. I refuse to have anything to do with a demon."

"I realize that. Now. You need to reconsider—"

"Bull-fucking-shit. I will do no such thing. No good will come out of demons ruling the Agency or Earth or whatever. No good. You used to know the truth."

David reacts as if Smythe slapped him, jerking back a step. "Chuck doesn't want to rule Earth."

"As your son said, bull-fucking-shit." I shake my head. "Have you lost your ever-loving mind? Demons want to rule humans. They consider us beneath them."

A single headshake negates my words. "Maybe for most demons, but not Chuck. He promised—"

"I don't give a shit what he promised, Dad. You can't make deals with the devil."

"They're winning this war." David gestures at me. "There aren't enough *Justitians*. It's only a matter of time before the demons win. And Chuck promised me money for Sara. I get money to take care of your mother and I'm on the winning side. Come with us, son. Join us and we will win the battle."

"By killing all the *Justitians* and mages?" Smythe shakes his head. "I think not."

"You fail to see the end game. We aren't killing all the *Justitians*. With Gin's bracelet, we can control them all. Maybe even with Gin intact."

Oh, how nice of him to leave me in one piece. Talk about generous. Although I'm assuming his "gift" only works if I agree with his plan.

And surprise, surprise, I'm right.

"Chuck claims Gin's *justitia* is the most powerful and will control the others. She's different," he glances at me like I'm a bug in an experiment, "so maybe she'll go along with us?"

I shake my head. No way. He glares.

"I might be a newbie to this *Justitian* gig, but even I know not to believe a demon. Chuck's playing you. Or should I call him Mammon?"

A pleased smile turns David's lips. "Very impressive. You're smarter than I gave you credit for."

"Thanks. But we have a bigger problem."

Smythe gives me a puzzled look as what feels like butterflies brush against my mind. His eyes widen for a split second before he once again faces his dad.

"What's Chuck planning to do to Eloise and T?"

"We thought to turn T, but Chuck will kill Eloise."

"Not if I can help it." Smythe slashes a hand through the air and David drops unconscious to the ground.

I squeak, jumping back in surprise. "What the hell?"

Smythe squats next to his father, checking for a pulse. "Sleeping spell. He wasn't expecting such a low-level spell. It won't last long. Help me tie him up."

"With what?" But the words no sooner leave my mouth than Smythe has conjured two strands of ropes. "How'd you do that?"

I grab a rope and tie David's ankles together.

"Eloise keeps rope by her front door. Don't ask. I pulled it from her apartment to here." He finishes tying David's wrists and stands, helping me to my feet.

"And here I thought you created it from thin air."

"Don't be ridiculous. A mage can't create an object out of thin air." He grabs my hand and speed-walks to the elevator. "T should be okay for now. We're going to get Eloise out first."

"According to T, Chuck is in an interrogation room with Eloise. Can I kill him this time?"

He leans against the wall of the elevator and rubs the bridge of his nose. "Yeah. I know from Dad how far his influence goes. It's bad. About half the mages are under his thrall, including Samantha."

"And that's a surprise?"

He barks a laugh. "Yeah. I mean no." Laughter fades as a serious look covers his face. "We have until the elevator stops to come up with a plan."

"They're probably expecting us."

"Chuck will be, but according to what I read in Dad's mind, he also hasn't made a decision about whether or not we pose a threat. Dad convinced him, or at least he believed he convinced him, to give us a chance. More like me a chance, but still."

"He also made it sound like they were considering keeping me alive. Since blowing me up with my house worked out so well."

"Yep. So the plan is to act like we are on Chuck's side. Keep him off balance. I'll cast a spell to keep your *justitia* hidden and hope he doesn't notice it's a sword. Once we're in the interrogation room, I'll dismantle the cameras—"

"I thought they were spell proof?"

"I said dismantle, not wipe clean. I'll dismantle the cameras and you'll kill Chuck. Maybe Eloise can help, maybe she can't, but we're going to take that damn demon out or die trying."

I nod. Sounds like a plan to me.

Except for the dying part.

Chapter Twenty-One

My *justitia* morphs into a sword as soon as the elevator doors open to the basement. With a quiet tone, Smythe wraps the sword in an invisibility spell. We head toward the interrogation rooms, our shoes thudding against the linoleum floor. The strong scent of cleaning products hangs in the air, a choking miasma. Several demon-trail-wrapped mages line the corridors. I swallow. Were they like Smythe, covered in demonic essence due to casual contact with Chuck, or were they his willing henchmen?

Damn it. How am I supposed to tell who's on Team Chuck?

A familiar presence brushes against my mind. *T! We're here. Gonna get Eloise first. You still okay?*

Yep. So far they've left me alone. Go kill the demon, Gin.

That's the plan.

I refuse to tell him about the 'or die trying' part of the plan. He's angry enough already. But at least he's okay. For now. One less thing to worry about.

Smythe nods to the mages who return the gesture. "We heard Chuck captured the demon. Which room?"

"Demon's in room four." One of the mages answers. "The human is in room two, but we don't think he knows anything. Chuck said not to disturb him."

If they thought it strange Eloise was being called a demon, they keep it to themselves. I tamp down the impulse to slam my fist into their jaws. How could they have worked with Eloise for years and not be enraged over her being called a demon?

I guess that answers my earlier question if they're on Team Chuck or not.

Smythe heads to room four. "Chuck wants us in there."

"He said—"

"I said, he wants us in there."

The mages nod, eyes glassy. The same one who spoke earlier replies. "You're right. Go on in."

Amazing. The compulsion spell works on mages. I'm assuming these mages aren't as powerful as mine.

I draw in a deep breath as Smythe slams open the door to interrogation room four. We step inside and I kick the door shut with my foot. Chuck stands with his back to us, one hand raised to strike the body slumped against the table. He straightens as we walk in. Eloise remains half-in and half-out of her chair, her chained hands keeping her from falling to the floor.

A growl echoes around the room. It takes me a second to realize the noise comes from me. I take a step forward as Chuck turns to see who walked in on him. Claw marks streak down his face, leaving bloody welts. Small cuts slash through his expensive white silk shirt, staining it a deep crimson.

Son of a bitch. He hurt my friend. At least she got in several strikes before he knocked her unconscious.

A sinister smile spreads across Chuck's lips. "I see you don't believe she's the demon."

"You know we know who the true demon is."

So much for going in pretending to be on Chuck's side. Smythe steps in front of me, as if he's afraid I'm going to start a fight before we talk to Chuck.

And he's right. Restraining the anger vibrating my limbs requires too much energy. I want to set free a round of *Justitian* whoop-ass.

A preternatural stillness overtakes Chuck, the same expression seen on a pissed-off Zagan. Demonic. A dead giveaway of what he is for no human can replicate the posture.

A sigh escapes his lips. "I hoped it wouldn't come to this."

"Did you truly think no one would find you out?"

"That was the plan." Chuck's eyes narrow. "How did you find out? In all the years I've been here, my spell worked without a problem."

Smythe shrugs, clearly not wanting to give away our secret. Chuck continues to peer at my mage like he's an ape in the zoo, previously thought dumb until the primate exhibits an intelligent behavior.

"The only way my spell could be broken is if a demon offered the counterspell. And very few demons know that particular spell. All the ones who know it are dead. So tell me, boy, what bargain with which demon did you make?"

"If they're all dead, what does it matter?"

"Oh, it matters. As I said, the demons who know that particular spell are dead, either by my hand or a *Justitian's*. Again, how did you learn of it?"

"Why Eloise?" Instead of answering, Smythe counters with his own question. His fingers flex, small flickers of blue light flashing from his nails.

Never seen him do that before. Was he mad or

getting ready for a magical fireworks showdown?

Chuck glances at the injured healer. "She was close to discovering who I was despite my spell. She thwarted me at every turn. Stole your *justitia*." He waves a hand at me. "Hid *Justitians* so I wouldn't kill them. An all-around trouble-maker. It seemed only fitting. I'd hoped you would have brought her in, but I see you tried to play me. It didn't work. She'll die. Then you will. Then the *Justitian*." Again, he waves a dismissive hand my direction.

Kill demon. The eerie voice of the *justitia* sounds in my head. *Kill demon now!*

Don't worry. Once Smythe lets me, I will.

And why wasn't he letting me? Right. Information. Instead of information, my mage seems to be more eager to get into a pissing match with the demon.

I side with the *justitia*. Chuck needs to go into the headless afterlife STAT.

Unfortunately, before I can move forward, Smythe holds out a hand to stop me. Sure, I could push past him, but Eloise winking at us catches my attention and stops me in my tracks.

Does the wink mean she's okay? Her eyes close as Chuck turns to glare at her. I try to blank my face so as not to give away the fact she's not unconscious. At least I'm assuming she's not unconscious but pretending.

To what end? Or was the wink accidental and she's worse than she looks? And damn, but she looks awful. Blood cakes her lips, trickles from her nose. Bruises line the pale skin of her face, greens and purples fading to yellow.

Wait a minute. Were the bruises fading? I snap my attention to Chuck. Judging from his gotcha expression,

I'm a second too late.

"It takes a lot to kill a nephilim." He cracks his fingers. "You can chop off their heads, but where's the fun in that?"

"You had fun cutting up that minion." I glare, ignoring Smythe's waving hand.

"You knew all along." He glances at my wrist. "If you know, why do you not have a sword?"

I raise my arm, looking at my wrist as if I can't see the sword. The spell hiding the *justitia* from view doesn't prohibit me from seeing it. I plaster on a surprised look while moseying toward the demon.

"Gin." Ignoring the warning in Smythe's voice, I stop a foot from Chuck.

"What do you know? It's not a sword. Or is it?" I swing, aiming for his neck, but the demon hops out of the way in a blur of movement.

No problem. My *justitia* can control my body to move as fast.

In theory.

In practice. Kill demon.

With those words, the entity takes control of my limbs, whirling me into a blur of parries and thrusts. But Chuck's faster, stronger, more powerful. His fist strikes me from nowhere, throwing me out of super-speed to land on one of Smythe's invisi-mats.

Thank god for my mage.

And thank god for my *justitia,* who blocks the pain receptors turning my jaw into a screaming ball of fire.

I hop to my feet, circle the demon while looking for a hint of his next move. He smiles. I glare. We circle each other until his back is to the table, giving me a view of Eloise. She sits upright, shaking out hands

Smythe freed from the cuffs. I wasn't imaging things earlier. Her bruises are barely existent.

My shock gives Chuck the opportunity he needs to get in a punch. Damn it. I really need to pay attention during a fight instead of sightseeing and daydreaming.

I land on another invisible cushion, right in time to see Chuck focus on Eloise. She raises her hands and a bolt of lightning slams into Chuck.

Day-um. Remind me not to piss her off.

Chuck stumbles back a step as smoke circles his chest. Instead of dying like a normal person, he bats a hand and the smoke dissipates. Right. Because he's not a person and demons are never normal. While he's off-guard, I spring to my feet, arm drawn for a blow. But instead of striking Eloise, he casts some sort of spell sending us all flying backward.

This time no invisible cushy mat greets my flight and I slam into the wall with a thud. Pain blossoms along my back, but the *justitia* overrides my nervous system, eliminating the ache. At least nothing feels broken. Two other thuds sound as Eloise and Smythe smack into the walls. Chuck remains standing, hands loose at his sides, a shiver-inducing grin curving his lips.

"Do you really think you can take me on? I'm more powerful than the three of you combined. You will die."

Demons and their constant threats of death. You'd think after all the millennia they've lived, they would've come up with some better lines.

On the other hand, most fights consisting of human versus demon end with a demon victory.

Not this time.

This time I have Zagan's red energy as a backup. But I want to kill this damn demon without demonic assistance. I'll use Zagan's energy boost if I start to lose the battle. I might be down but I'm not out.

Yet.

"You know what they say." Smythe struggles to his feet, his grimace a clear indication his flight into the wall hurt more than mine. "Pride goeth before a fall."

Chuck barks a laugh, his attention remaining on my mage. Which allows me to stalk toward him with the speed of a turtle. Slow and steady. Slow and steady. As long as he keeps his attention elsewhere, I stand a chance of winning this battle. Despite Smythe's gaze locked on the demon, I know he understands my strategy.

His assistance comes in the form of an overactive mouth.

"You think I'm kidding. I'm not." Smythe glares as I creep closer.

Two steps. One step. I draw my arm back for the killing blow.

"You are right. You aren't kidding. Pride does go before a fall. Just not mine."

With those words he spins, arm blocking my swing. Smythe lobs an energy ball at the demon, as does Eloise, but the demon shakes off the explosion of energy, his fingers wrapping around my throat.

My vision dims. I ram my knee upward. He might be demonic but even demons have balls. Chuck only flinches at a strike that would've crippled a minion. On the plus side, his grip lessens enough for me to draw in a gasp of air. Energy balls from Smythe and Eloise continue to pound his back, singe his white shirt, and have abso-fucking-lutely no effect.

Great.

And then I'm airborne, arms and legs pinwheeling as I smack into the wall. The *justitia* acts fast, shutting down my pain receptors before pain blossoms. Unfortunately, the entity can't control the dizziness making my head swim.

I blink, focusing on the fight. Eloise throws energy ball after energy ball, unerring in her accuracy. Which makes me wonder how she manages that trick being blind. Sure, she claims she can see out of others' eyes if she's emotionally close to them, but that "sight" means she doesn't stumble over a moved table. Then again, what do I know? I can't even see straight at the moment.

Smythe fires a blue bolt of energy, smacking Chuck in the side, causing the demon to stumble. Eloise follows up with another round of energy balls while Smythe starts chanting in a language that sounds suspiciously like Latin. Chuck lets out a roar, clasping his hands over his ears. Was he really bothered more by the spell than the energy balls?

Using the wall as a crutch, I shove upright. Black spots line my periphery. Or maybe those were due to the flashes of light turning the room into a strobing disco ball. White light explodes from Chuck as smoke swirls around him, hiding him from view.

When the smoke dissipates, it's no longer Chuck standing before us. It's Mammon. The same demon who sent a minion to burn down my house. Who sent minions to a financial advisor's office. Who, undoubtedly, is behind the payments coming in to the Agency.

Who bellows a war cry.

Lucky for us, Smythe's reveal-spell seems to prohibit the demon from moving. A trick I'm certain won't last long.

Smythe holds out a hand to me, a warning to stay put. No problem. I'm not convinced I could make it the three steps and a swing to create a headless demon.

"What was your end goal?"

Chuck/Mammon shakes his head. "You think to hold me, boy? You think your measly spell will bind me?"

"Answer the question." Eloise steps to Smythe's side.

"Filthy half-breed. You should never have left me."

Say what? I blink, the dancing spots in my peripheral vision vanishing under a wave of what-the-hell.

"Wealth isn't everything." A ball of energy sits in the palm of her hand as Eloise glares at the demon. "I should have known it was you who possessed the Agency."

"Ah, yes, bitch, you should have. It was all for you. At first, anyway. I followed you here, you know. Assumed this body," he draws a hand down his chest, as if he doesn't realize he no longer looks like Chuck, "pretended to be a mage, and snuck right in. The leaders were dumb. Couldn't even tell a demon from a mage."

"Was it the forget-spell?" A small bead of sweat trickles down Smythe's cheek.

Maybe it wasn't the reveal-spell holding Chuck/Mammon in place, maybe it was Smythe working a spell even as he spoke.

Mammon's eyes narrow. "Of course it was the spell, you idiot. That and humans see what they want to see. They want to see a mage, they see a mage. Stupid sheep. But I could lead them and lead them I did. I changed appearances over the years so as not to rouse suspicion and soon I was the leader."

The cadence of his speech increases as he gets into telling his story.

"I was the best leader ever, the best. But it wasn't good enough. I had long since forgotten about her," he waves a dismissive hand to Eloise, "and moved on to better things. Why not grow the funds of the Agency? Of course I would use those funds. Don't you like the golden chandeliers? The expensive furnishings? This place thrived under my hand."

"We found the deposits from some of the largest companies and biggest billionaires in the nation." A fine tremor runs through Smythe.

Mammon smiles. "Ah yes. A shakedown, I believe they call it. My minions find dirt on them, tell me, and one blackmail later the money comes pouring in. It's amazing what the rich will do to hide their sins. And what magic will do to cover my trail. No one realized it was me calling the shots. No one cared. And so many good little mages were turned quite easily to my agenda. Give them a little money, a little power, allow them to let loose a little rage, and they are all mine. Forever. For not only have I amassed control of the Agency, but I am in control of Hell. No one else can rule but me."

"That's what you think." I step forward, shutting down his tirade.

Mammon turns to me, shaking his head. "Silly girl.

I am the last of the demons who are able to control Hell."

"That's what you think." A grin curves my lips. The expression on his face, confidence turning to doubt, makes a little bud of happiness grow deep within me. Just wait, dumbass.

He raises a brow, condescension overthrowing his doubt. "Enough talk. You have what you wanted. You can die with knowledge."

With a roar, he throws his arms out to the sides, releasing a wave of energy that knocks us, once again, against the wall. This time the energy holds us in place, unable to break free.

No good, no good! My *justitia* screams in my head.

No shit, Sherlock. Do something!

While the *justitia* runs through options, or disappears into silence, I'm not sure which, the demon laughs a soul-shuddering cackle as he turns in a slow circle.

"Who to start with first? Hmm. The *Justitian.* The mage? The filthy half-breed? Decisions, decisions."

I try to yank my arm free. And fail. I can breathe and roll my eyes. Nothing else on my body moves. Judging from the panic in Smythe's eyes he has the same problem. Mammon blocks Eloise from view, but I assume she also struggles in vain against his spell.

"I'll choose the filthy half-breed."

Before I can blink, he's shot an energy ball at Eloise, dropping her prone on the ground.

He rubs his hands together, evil villain style. "Don't be jealous. She was almost free of my spell. And the blast didn't hurt her like it will you. So, who's next?" He looks at me then Smythe. "Ah. David's idiotic son. I'll do the man a favor. He'll only miss you for a little while."

I call bullshit on that. David might be working for Mammon and be a world-class asshole, but the man loves his son.

Another round of struggling gets me nowhere. Can't move, can't talk, can't save Smythe. Oh god, I have to watch Mammon kill my friend and lover.

Panic ricochets through my system, spiking my adrenaline, causing me to…remain stuck against the wall. Anger surges. The entity along my nerves begins to chant, the rhythmic language a distraction from Smythe's impending death.

Mammon draws back his arm in slow motion, a flame of energy sitting in his palm. Time slows as he releases the fiery ball.

"No!" The door to the room slams open, David dashing inside.

He throws himself between his son and the flare of energy, taking the blow to his left shoulder and upper chest. Smythe's eyes widen as he screams silently, the sound echoing in my mind, a cry of anguish. A nonplussed expression darts across Mammon's face as he stares at the downed David.

Did David sacrifice himself for his son?

The entity inside me continues to chant, faster and faster, as a purple glow expands around my body. The thing screams the last word, the purple glow flashing so bright I close my eyes in defense.

And then I'm free, my feet sliding to the floor, my arms tingling with movement. Using Mammon's distraction, I draw back my arm, rushing the demon. He turns at the last moment, but my blade strikes his upper arm, cutting deep. With a roar, he jumps out of my way, stumbling into the table.

A cold breeze dashes into the room, surrounding me like a freezing hug. Mammon's eyes widen as he straightens, his gaze fixed behind me. Transparent shapes swirl into the room. Ghosts.

Only one person I know who can call ghosts and he's chained in the next room.

T?

That son of a bitch is going down for good.

I step to the side and glance quickly over my shoulder. Somehow T freed himself, called a bunch of ghosts, and now stands in the doorway, ready to whoop some demon ass.

Bring. It. On.

Mammon recovers, his what-the-hell expression morphing into anger. Ghosts swirl around him, but unlike Perdix—the despair demon T fought with ghosts—Mammon ignores the spirits. His gaze fixates on me. Before I can blink, a red energy ball flies through the air at me.

Oh, shit. I tried to fight this fight on my own, but it's evident the only way to kill Mammon is to use the energy Zagan gave me. This fight has gone on long enough. Time to end it. Time for Mammon to die.

I shove the *justitia* in front to ward off the flying red death. The energy ball strikes my sword as T's ghosts dive through Mammon. Concentrating on the demonic energy flaming along my *justitia*, I reach inside for another round of demonic energy. Zagan's energy. The exact thing he gave me to win this fight.

The *justitia* absorbs Mammon's red power blast, mingles it with a little of Zagan's, and with a flick of my wrist throws it back to the demon of greed.

The strike nails him in the chest. He flies backward, landing on the table. More ghosts dive through him. This time he swats at the see-through buggers. I step closer, arm drawn for a killing blow.

When the ghosts vanish on a thud.

A thud?

"Get away from him, bitch!"

At Samantha's voice, I glance over my shoulder. Shit. Looks like she knocked out my twin. Double shit. All my fighting buddies are down for the count.

Or stuck against the wall.

Same thing.

Who to fight first? The demon or his pawn?

"You don't smell like a minion, Samantha."

"That's because I'm not. Minions aren't the only ones who believe a demon is in the right."

"Yeah, and those people belong in the psych ward."

Her eyes narrow. Right. Enough talk. Time for action.

Working on the theory that if the demon dies, so will the sympathizer, I whirl, letting the entity inside me blur my movements as I swing at Mammon.

Unfortunately, the damn demon sees my move and reacts. On the plus side, my blade slices deep into his deltoid. Black demon blood streams from both of his arms. If only he used a sword instead of tossing energy balls like they were water balloons, I'd win this fight.

Samantha fires a power-blast at me. I catch it on the flat of my blade and toss the energy ball back to her. Unlike the demon, she doesn't move fast enough, and my aim is true. Her face holds pain and surprise as she drops to the floor. Is she dead or unconscious? I don't have time to check since another wave of energy balls are thrown my way.

I dodge one and catch another on my blade, reflecting it back to Mammon.

"How are you doing that?" He snarls. "*Justitians* can't control demonic energy."

"I'd tell you, but then I'd have to kill you. Oh wait. I'm going to kill your slimy ass anyway."

I swing. He dodges. I catch another energy ball and fling it back at him.

And then the temperature in the room drops as a thick, white fog of spirits surrounds us. Mammon's eyes widen. He sucks in a breath and swallows hard.

His voice escapes in a low growl. "How are you doing that?"

"I'm not." My lips curl into a shit-eating grin. "Say good-bye, bitch. Zagan sends his regards."

I charge him as the ghosts dart through his middle. He screams, swatting at the spirits, but manages to deflect my blow.

"Impossible! I sent my willing servant to hunt him down and ensure he died. Zagan's dead."

"Is he really?"

Willing servant? Does he mean Samantha? I start to glance to my prone nemesis but think better of taking my eyes off the irate demon. Good decision since he tosses an energy ball before my gaze fully returns to him. The thing fizzles during flight, dying due to a lack of strength. Which makes it easy to avoid.

Neener neener, stupid demon.

Spirits continue to dive through his body as we circle each other. Mammon swats at them but keeps his red-eyed focus on me.

"You killed him!" Spittle bubbles in the corners of his mouth. Red blossoms on his cheeks as his fists clench. A fine tremor shakes his arms. "Samantha said you killed him!"

"Ever heard of illusions? Zagan is the master of deceit, after all."

He shakes his head. "It's against the covenant. He can't kill me! We swore not to kill each other."

Interesting. But the answer pops into my mind, thanks to the *justitia's* memories. Another devious grin coats my lips.

"You swore not to kill each other. You didn't swear not to have another kill you. Like you sent Samantha to kill Zagan."

Mammon's eyes narrow, then widen. Then narrow. He roars and charges, but I'm ready for him. He's weakened from T's ghosts, from the cuts on his arms, from the knowledge Zagan one upped him. This time he's not as strong.

But I am. I still have a good deal of Zagan's energy. Energy I pull to the surface, direct onto the *justitia*, and slash at the demon.

The blade slices through his neck, clean and neat. His body and head drop in two different directions, surprise the last expression to hit his face. With a pop, he vanishes, nothing but black silt left where he lay.

A thud reverberates against the floor as the spell holding Smythe against the wall releases. He dashes to his father, his *nonononono* cry tearing at my heart as he kneels beside David.

I want to comfort him, to pull him into my arms, to let him know everything will be okay. Which is a lie.

Everything will not be okay. We might have killed Mammon, but there was so much more to do at the Agency. If Mammon spoke true about half the staff being devoted to him, then a huge problem still remains.

A wave of dizziness strikes. My breath saws in and out of my lungs as I work to drag in air. Fuzzy black spots line my periphery, waiting to drag me into unconsciousness.

I lean over, hands resting on my knees, fighting the lights-out. The temperature of the room seems to rise. Or maybe being dizzy makes me flushed.

T pats my back, answering my curiosity. A definite rise in room temperature, since he must have sent the ghosts to wherever they stay when not helping to kill demons.

"You okay?" He leans over, peering into my eyes.

"Yeah. I think. Eloise—"

"Oh, fuck."

And with another pat on the back, he's gone, rushing to his healer girlfriend, leaving me alone to drag in air.

Why am I so dizzy?

The reason dawns under a quick dash of pain, as if the *justitia* removed its restraints on my pain receptors. I guess the flight into the wall damaged something but the *justitia* and a good dose of adrenaline coupled with demonic energy made the injury not seem as bad.

Damn it. I hate getting hurt.

The injury realization gives me permission to butt-plant it on the floor. I'm not looking like a wimp, I'm taking care of myself.

Yeah, right. If I was taking care of myself, I

wouldn't be fighting demons.

Demons fun to fight. Bad demons need to die. You killed bad greedy demon.

Thank you for your help.

Me help. Me like you best of all Justitians. *Except first wearer. You remind me of her. Me like you.*

I like you too. I'm going to close my eyes now.

Uh-oh. You close eyes no good.

But its voice trails away, fades into the distance, into the fog surrounding my mind.

Relief drenches me. Safe. All who matter to me are safe and relatively unharmed. Except for Eloise and she won't stay injured for long. I'm just going to relax for a minute, no more. Then I'll get up and help defeat the demon's remaining followers. In a minute. A minute…

I succumb to the darkness.

Chapter Twenty-Two

I wake to the rush of the infirmary, to the quick thuds of running footsteps, to the cries for assistance. Antiseptic mingles with lemon-scented cleaning products, both scents masking the odor of bodily fluids. I know where I am before I even open my eyes. The question being, what happened to cause this rush?

I open my eyes. First thing I notice is yep, I'm in an infirmary bed, the curtain pulled around to give me privacy. The second thing I see is T sitting in a chair next to the bed, the chair pulled so close his knees touch the mattress. A shadow of a beard scratches his cheeks. How long have I been out and why hasn't he shaved?

He grabs my hand. "Thank god you're awake."

I swallow. Twice. My mouth feels like the Sahara. "What happened?"

"You killed Mammon."

"Yeah. And you helped." Memories of the fight swirl through my mind. "How did you get free?"

A grin curves his lips. "Called the ghosts. They broke the chains."

"Seriously?"

"Cross my heart and all that shit."

Who knew ghosts could break chains. Something to keep in mind in case I ever find myself shackled to one of the interrogation room tables.

A more important thought crosses my mind. "How

long have I been out?"

"A day." He passes me a glass of water with a straw and I take a sip as he talks. "It's Thursday. You probably would've woken up faster, but Eloise couldn't heal you."

"How is she?"

"Fine now. Physically anyway." His jaw tightens. "I'd kill that bastard again if I could."

"Yeah. Me too. What about Smythe?"

He pats my hand as he takes back the glass of water. "His father died. He's really upset. And while you've been out things around here have gone to hell in a handbasket, no pun intended. The mages who didn't follow Mammon have been hunting the ones who did. It's not quite half and half, there're more good guys than bad, but a war is being fought in this building."

My eyes widen. I shouldn't be surprised. We knew this would happen. Would have to happen. Cleaning house is the only way to eradicate Mammon's influence. "Is that why this place is hopping?"

"Yeah." He nods. "Smythe and Eloise are leading the hunting parties. She's recovered enough to hunt the bad guys but doesn't think she's able to heal. Takes too much energy or something. She made the second-best healer fix you up."

I flex my feet. "Maybe I should help."

"Hell no." He pokes a finger my direction. "You are under orders to lie right there and heal. No helping allowed."

"What happened to Samantha?"

"You killed her."

"She was working for Mammon. Knew who he was."

He shakes his head. "Total bitch."

He's got that right. While I should feel bad for killing a human, I don't. Samantha was corrupt. She deserved her death.

Dropping his hand, I sit upright. A pillow fluff later and I lean back a little short of breath. Clearly the second-best healer was nowhere close to possessing Eloise's ability to heal me good as new. If Eloise had worked her healing magic on me, I'd be up and fighting.

"Who's winning?"

"The good mages, who else? Without their demonic backer, the followers are either claiming he enthralled them—which he very well might have done—or saying they made the biggest mistake of their lives. Those are the ones who aren't straight up fighting back. The apologizing ones are getting sent to the interrogation rooms. The others are getting killed. Too much demon in them."

I shiver. "That's sad. I always knew this place had something off about it since my *justitia* always thought a demon lived here and was puzzled when it couldn't figure out who or where that demon was. But it's sad so many mages went over to the demon side."

"It's amazing what a little money or power can do." T shakes his head. "Make a person turn the other way. Compromise morals. See nothing wrong because it's your guy. Or demon as the case may be."

"Even Smythe's father was working with Mammon. And he was the boss of the mages."

"Yeah. You'd think David would've known better."

"He wanted to help his comatose wife get better.

Mammon promised to heal her."

T's eyes widen. "Really? Did he do it?"

"No."

"See? You can't trust a demon."

Unless it's Zagan. Geez Louise, I'm in trouble if I can think that with a straight face. I swallow. Topic change.

"How long do you think this fight is going to go on?"

He shrugs, either not picking up on my change of topic or deciding to let it lie. "It looks to me like it's almost over. People are still coming in here but not as fast as they were. Smythe stopped by earlier today and Eloise came around a couple of hours ago. They both seemed to think all the truly bad mages have been caught. The rest need to be interviewed to determine whether or not they can be trusted."

"How can they trust them to work as mages?"

"I have no idea." A half-shrug wiggles his shoulders. "I couldn't."

"Me either. Maybe they'll send the truth-tellers to rehab or something."

"Rehab?" He shakes his head.

"So, how's the *Justitian* who helped start this fight?" A healer in white scrubs with a blue circle on the breast pocket steps into the room, interrupting our speculation.

The tall, brunette woman smiles at me, concern written on her face. Her words, though, scrape like fingernails down the chalkboard of my spine. Was she one of the bad mages? Or just trying to be funny and not hitting her mark?

Probably a failed attempt at a joke. Smythe and

Eloise would have cleaned out the infirmary first thing ensuring the healers were on their side.

I shrug. "Still a little tired, but clearly better than I was. Thank you."

She steps to my side, takes my wrist, and closes her eyes. After a long pause, her eyes open, a smile curving her lips. "You're much better than when you came in."

"If I promise not to fight, will you let me out of here?"

"Done." She reaches to the foot of my bed, hands me a plastic bag. "Here're your clothes. Let me know if you need anything else or if you feel worse. Other than that, you're free to go."

Giving my foot a pat, she opens the curtain, closing it behind her. T points to the bag gripped in my hands.

"Your phone's been ringing."

My brow wrinkles as I pull out my phone. The time reads a few minutes after six in the evening. Four new voicemails show in the notifications bar. I unlock the screen, tap the voicemail icon and hit play. The first message is from the detective working my house fire case. Once again, he confirms arson resulted in my fire—as if I didn't already know—and informs me I can go back and try to pull out possessions.

I sigh. It's probably easier to replace everything except I'm not sure what's going to happen since Mammon is dead. Will the new Agency leaders agree to pay me? Do I even want them to? Will I go back to my job?

Oh shit.

Thinking of Blue Forest Emergency Department makes me realize I had an appointment this morning with my counselor, Kathy Funk. An appointment I missed. Crapola. If I don't show for those appointments, then I'm out of a job.

The thought no longer gives me a panic attack. I'm not sure if that's a good thing or a bad one.

I tap on the next message. Sure enough, it's from Kathy's office stating I missed my appointment and requesting I call to reschedule. Double sigh.

The third call is from Will letting me know he's okay and wondering what happened. I'll call him back in a few.

The last message is from an unknown number. Great. A spam call. I almost delete it, but something urges me to listen. My spine stiffens as Zagan's deep voice fills my ears.

"We need to meet. Call me." He leaves his number. A sharp click indicates the end of the call.

Not much for phone conversations, my demon.

I exit out of voice mail and glance up as T raises a brow.

"The detective confirmed the house fire was arson. Will called. And I missed a counseling session."

"Is that bad?" A wrinkle forms between his eyebrows.

"Don't know. Probably. Right now, I'm not so sure I care."

He shrugs as he shoves his chair back a foot. "Know what you mean." Standing, he gives me a half-grin. "Get dressed. I'll wait for you."

As soon as he ducks through the privacy curtain, I throw off the sheet. Putting on dirty clothes wasn't a pleasant experience, but if I could figure out how to get into Smythe's apartment, I could change into my spare set. I sit on the bed to yank on my boots and send out a

SOS to Smythe.

Smythe?

A couple of seconds later, relief floods my mind. *Gin! You okay?*

Yep. You?

Yeah, but this place is a holy mess.

I refrain from saying 'I told you so.' Go me. *I'm sorry about your dad. How are you holding up?*

Tension drifts through my mind. *Thanks. I'd rather not talk about it right now.*

Okay then. As he wishes. *You know I'm here if you need to talk.*

Yeah. It's appreciated.

Since our mental link goes silent, I change topics to my pressing current problem.

I need to change clothes, so I need to get into your apartment.

A sense of relief flows through our link. *No problem. We've rounded up the last of the demon followers. I can meet you there.*

Great. Thanks. See you soon.

He blocks our conversation as I stand onto wobbly, unused-for-a-day legs. Thank goodness he was fine and willing to meet me. Too bad he hadn't given me a key to his apartment, then I could get in myself. On the other hand, I'm not certain I could open a magically locked apartment even with the key.

I shake my head. Relationship problems.

As soon as I yank open the curtain, T looks me up and down, his lips twitching.

"You look like shit."

I roll my eyes. "Thanks. Glad you saved that comment for when I'm up and moving."

"What can I say? Looking like shit while lying in an infirmary bed is par for the course, right? Looking like shit while standing? Not so much."

I give him a little shove toward the elevator. Twin brothers, I swear. "Get on with you. Smythe's going to meet us at his apartment so I can change."

"Good move."

He dodges my attempted whack upside his head.

I call Will as we head to Smythe's apartment. He doesn't pick up, so I let him know I'm good, Mammon is dead, and I won't be in to work this week. Or ever. A fact I leave out of my message.

By the time we get to Smythe's apartment, my lover is leaning against the door. I give him a hug, squeezing his waist as we kiss. Ah. The longer I'm in his arms, the better I feel.

T clears his throat. "Enough already. I'm going blind over here."

Smythe steps back, dropping his arms from my waist as he stares at my twin. Who chuckles. I shake my head.

"Come on. I need to change."

Smythe turns to the door, holds his hand over the lock while muttering, then he punches a code into the keypad. With a snick, the lock releases and we step inside.

I head toward the bedroom, grab my spare set of clothes and hit the shower, leaving the men to themselves. The warm water feels good cascading down my body, so I stay a little longer than I should, until my skin wrinkles and steam fogs the mirror.

Taking a long shower after killing the big bad demon leaves me relaxed and ready for the next step.

Getting out of the Agency building to find Zagan.

Which shouldn't be a problem. Buildings have these newfangled things called doors, after all. Except this one. Supposedly the Agency looks like a boarded-up office building with enough enchantments to cause non-magical humans to ignore it. I wouldn't know, having only portalled in and out of the building.

If my memory serves, Smythe once told me the only way in and out of the building was through the white landing room. Of course, that was before he realized Eloise came and went as she pleased. At any rate, no one used the doors. As in no one used them because they didn't really exist.

Talk about violating fire codes.

I need to find a way out even though I know what Zagan wants. To congratulate me on killing Mammon. To tell me he's now the ruler of Hell. To try to persuade me to become his servant in truth.

Not happening on that last one.

I need to convince him to release me. I've served my purpose with him, he needs to remove his mark from my neck.

And the chances of him hopping on the Gin freedom wagon remain pretty much non-existent.

Damn it.

I flip on the fan, which does two things, defogs the mirror and masks my call to the demon of deceit. He answers on the first ring.

"Hello, Gin." His deep voice puckers my flesh into shivers of delight and fear. "And congratulations."

Yep, I was right. At least about him congratulating me on a demon-killing job well-done.

"Thanks. How did you know? And how did you

get my number?"

"I always know when a demon who made a pact with me dies. As for your number, I can function in this new technological world. I merely prefer face-to-face meetings. They're more personal, do you not think?"

And scary. Not like I'll mention my true feelings. "Sure. So you called to congratulate me? I suppose I should congratulate you. You're ruling Hell now, huh?"

His grin comes through in his words. "You are correct. I am the most powerful now. Control is mine. Thanks to you. We need to meet."

And, yep again, I guessed correctly.

"Do we? Can't you tell me on the phone?"

He sniffs. "No. It needs to be in person."

"For that personal touch."

"Of course. As I said."

I roll my eyes. Figures he'd want to meet in person. Then again, I want to end our pretend demon-servant relationship so maybe breakups should be done in person.

"Not sure if I can leave."

"Walk out the door."

"I'm pretty sure the doors are illusion."

"No, they are not. I am looking at your esteemed building even as we speak. Wards aplenty, but the doors are real. Warded, but real."

Well, that was a relief. I guess the place isn't violating as many fire code laws as I thought. More importantly, I can escape without using the landing room.

"Okay. I'll try to find out how to use them."

"Most doors require you to turn a knob or push a bar."

"Thanks, smartass." Geez Louise, did I actually insult a demon? What am I thinking? Make that not thinking.

A low chuckle fills my ear. "I will meet you in the Granary Burying Ground at 9 P.M. That's two hours, in case you are wondering. You should have plenty of time to discover how to find and open a door."

He hangs up before I can agree. Okay, then. Looks like I need to find a door. But how, without arousing suspicion? And where was this place?

A quick check on the phone pulls up the cemetery as one of the stops on the Freedom Trail. Great. Crowds. Actually, maybe not. The place closes at five. Okay, then. One problem solved. One more to go.

I finish in the bathroom, flip off the call-covering fan, and march into the living room. T and Smythe sit on the couch staring at the TV, although I'm not convinced either watch the show.

"Hey! Thanks for the use of the shower."

Smythe snaps his attention from the TV, a grin curving his lips. "As I said before, you're welcome to anything here."

I walk to the couch, pat his shoulder and flop in his lap.

"How's it going with the fight?"

He shakes his head. "I can't believe how many people followed Mammon knowingly. Including Dad." Sadness creeps into his eyes, although his voice remains steady. "We've rounded up everyone who knowingly followed a demon. We're trying to decide what to do with them."

"Aren't you killing them?" T asks.

Smythe shakes his head. "Only if they fight us."

"Oh. I thought you were killing them." A look of relief passes over T's face.

"Nope. We want to try to redeem the knowing followers. Many more followed Chuck, Mammon, without realizing he was a demon. It's a mess. Then there're half of us who didn't even notice a demon in our midst."

"He cast a spell." I squeeze his hand. "No one noticed. How do you think he stayed here so long?"

"Did you know he created the warding spells to exclude him?" Irritation crosses his face. "That way he could travel in and out without being detected. He even helped write the demon-finding computer program."

"Ah-ha. No wonder the thing hardly worked." I knew something was wrong with that program.

"I can't believe I didn't notice all the fishy things earlier." He shakes his lowered head.

I give his hand another squeeze. "Don't beat yourself up. For years, no one but Eloise realized a demon haunted the Agency."

"And me," T chimes in.

"You only knew because you talked to the ghost." I raise a brow.

"Same thing." He shrugs.

I shake my head. "Whatever. So, Smythe, what are you doing now?"

"Sitting here with a hot woman on my lap." His eyebrows waggle.

I roll my eyes. "Besides that. I mean, what did I interrupt for you to let me take a shower?"

"Oh." He shakes his head, his lips twisting. "Those of us not following Mammon are interviewing those who did. We're deciding what to do with those who followed him without realizing he was a demon. Most are regretful and horrified. Those we're probably going to let go with some counseling. It's the ones who didn't give a shit that we need to decide what to do about. I guess I need to get back to the interrogation rooms. They need my help."

"Is that where Eloise is?" T asks.

"Yeah. She's helping. She'll be back up here tonight."

Perfect. Hopefully what I'm about to ask will go unnoticed as to my true motivation.

"Since you both are going to be busy, you think I could go explore the city? I've never been to Boston outside of the Agency building."

Smythe and T raise brows. I blank my mind, knowing my expression won't give anything away. I'm too skilled a liar.

"Now? You want to leave now?" Smythe's what-the-hell expression morphs into pensiveness. Never a good sign.

I shrug. "What good am I going to be here? And the weather looks nice."

"It's chilly. You'll need a jacket."

"I can borrow one of yours."

A long pause ensues as he stares at me. No thoughts, no thoughts, no thoughts.

"Okay." He draws out the word with the speed of Southerner. "I can let you out. They have shut down the landing room, but I can lower the wards around the doors. I'll give you a pass to get back in."

"And here I thought those doors were just for looks."

His arm around my waist tightens as he stands,

letting my feet slide to the floor. "If it helps, I just learned they have passes to let in *Justitians* when they aren't with their mages." He gives another quick head shake. "I can't believe all the things around here I didn't realize."

I pat his arm.

"You coming?" He turns to T.

T's mouth opens. I shoot him a hard glare coupled with a telepathic command. *You need to stay.*

He blinks. Closes his mouth. Opens it to speak. "I guess I'll stay here."

Smythe gives me a sideways glance. I grin. Crap, did he hear me? Even if he did, maybe he'll think I want to walk by myself.

It could happen.

I try to paste an innocent expression on my face. After a narrowed-eyes pause, Smythe nods.

"Okay. Come on, Gin. I don't have much time." He grabs a jacket out of the coat closet and hands it to me. The leather wraps me in warmth as I shrug it on.

It fits. Like he bought it for me. I raise a brow. Smythe shrugs.

Thought you might like it.

I give Smythe a hug and a kiss on the cheek. *I love it. You're the best. Thank you.*

"I'll stay here. It's Thursday night football." T waves at the TV. "Have a good walk, Gin." *Where the fuck are you going?*

I'll explain later.

Fine. He flops on the couch, grabs the remote, and turns up the volume.

I follow Smythe to the elevator. Once we step inside, he pushes the down button. The ride is short and quiet. I refuse the think about my upcoming "walk" since Smythe has a nasty habit of eavesdropping. When the elevator doors open, we step into a hallway almost as void of gilt as the basement.

"Where are we?"

Smythe turns left. "One floor up from the basement. It's how you get out."

"In case of a fire, right?"

"Don't be ridiculous. The building is warded against fire." He rubs the bridge of his nose. "Or at least it was."

"Are you having to reset the wards?"

"We blocked off the entire building. I probably shouldn't let you out."

"I appreciate it. Sorry, I just need to get out of here."

"Understood. If I could leave, I would. It's not a problem to let you out because I can cut a door in the wards that will reseal. You need to be back here in an hour. Touch the door and it will open for you. If you're late, you'll be caught outside."

"Make it two hours. I've never been to Boston and want to see the sights."

"It's night. More of a bar scene at night."

"I'm just walking. No bars for me."

"Good."

We stop at what looks like the end of the hall, no doors, no windows, only a beige wall.

"Um, Smythe?"

He shakes his head. "Oh, ye of little faith."

Waving his hand in a circle, he speaks words from an ancient language. The wall shimmers with a blue light, a door appearing in the middle. Smythe turns the old-fashioned brass knob and shoves the door open.

A glow from the streetlights streams into the opening. Cars honk as people walk past the building, not bothering to look at us. I guess the spell to turn away prying eyes remains in effect.

"Remember. Two hours. I'll set the spell to open for you then."

"Thank you." I pull out my phone, check the time with him, and stick it back in my pocket. "I'll be here. I appreciate you letting me out."

"No problem. See you soon."

I step into the chilly air as he pulls the door shut. A pop rings in my ears, a pressurized sensation like flying in a plane, the spell sealing the building. At least the door remains visible.

I save the location of the Agency on my phone, then pull up the address to the Granary Burying Ground. According to the map, I'll need to speed walk in order to make our meeting. So much for sightseeing. Although if I make it to the cemetery early, maybe I can look around without anyone noticing. According to Google, Paul Revere is buried there.

Shoving my hands in the jacket's pockets, I hurry toward my destination, ignoring the exhaustion creeping in. If only Eloise had healed me, I wouldn't be so tired. But it's tolerable, so I continue with the fast pace. The crowds thin for a couple of blocks before growing thick again with bar hoppers and pedestrians. The breeze chills me. I'm used to warm weather, not cooler temperatures. As long as I walk fast, I should be okay.

Finally, I make it to the cemetery. The place reeks of an ancient aura overlaid with a tangible presence of spirits. A chill chases beads of sweat down my spine. Nothing moves, not even the breeze. Laughter sounds nearby, but this place is deserted. Not that I blame the partiers for taking another route. I'm equally creeped out.

A black, iron fence surrounds the cemetery with a tall, Egyptian-style granite gateway in the middle. Four concrete steps lead to closed iron gates. Taking a deep breath, I reach for the gate, only to have it swing inward on well-oiled hinges. My heart hops behind my ribs as I release a gasp.

Calm down, Gin. Nothing to see here.

Shadows rustle under ancient trees, creeping across the old stone markers. A chill rushes down my spine. Definitely not the weather spooking me.

My *justitia* rattles against my wrist, doing its version of the happy dance, which means Zagan has arrived. Someplace.

I step inside the gate, turning to shut it. But before my fingers touch the metal, the thing closes without a sound. Great. I'm going to need to see a cardiologist for my heart palpitations.

"Hello, Gin." Zagan's deep voice sounds from one of the shadows surrounding a nearby tree.

My feet move toward the sound on their own volition. Because I'm damn sure if I was thinking clearly my feet would be pounding down the street away from this creepy-ass cemetery.

"I thought you'd like to meet me here. In a place similar to where you first needed my help."

My voice escapes thin and reedy. A real confidence booster. "I've never needed your help."

Which is a lie. Ironic. Seeing how I'm speaking

with the demon of lies and deceit. Then again, we've been through this. I know he's been helping me for longer than the time I've worn the *justitia*. Way longer. Like most of my life.

Double dog damn it.

I don't need his mark on my neck to tell me I am his.

How the hell am I going to get free?

He chuckles. "You lie. I like that in a person."

"Yeah, yeah. Demon of deceit and all. You won. What do you want from me?"

"You."

"Come again?"

He sighs, walking until he stops a foot away. His low-pitched voice strokes against my flesh. "You. I want you."

I want to step away from him, but my traitorous feet won't move. I clear my throat, trying to make my voice sound tough instead of its current small, scared tone. "Why?" Why? Why is the only word I can say? What the hell is wrong with me?

Never mind. My voice and brain might not work, but I can see in front of me just fine.

"You belong to me. You know this. Your blood has called to me for years. We can rule Hell together." He strokes the silver links of my *justitia*, taking care not to touch my skin. The entity along my nerves preens as if he stroked her.

A spine-shivering thought pops into my mind. Oh geez. I really should learn to be more observant.

"You slept with the gnome-like creature you killed to create the bracelets?"

He smiles. "Ah. Did she tell you this?"

I shake my head. *Whatever you do, don't give me memories of the two of you together. Total yuck.*

The entity chuckles, vibrating my nerves. *Me no tell.*

Thank god.

"I guessed. How could you kill her?"

Sadness crosses his face. "We each had to give up something we loved. The spell would not have worked otherwise."

"But you deceived the others into working a spell with you."

"No," he shakes his head, all remnants of sadness disappearing. "I did not. We agreed to rule Hell together. All thirteen of us. But when the human women escaped our bonds, two of us were killed. Then others over the years. That's when I worked out a plan to rid Hell of the remaining demons. I could not kill them, but nothing in our pact said I couldn't have them killed. I put into motion a plan to eliminate my competitors. If I hadn't done this, others would have."

"You sure about that?"

He smiles. "Why do you think Mammon took over the Agency?"

"Why didn't he turn the *Justitian* who wore his bracelet into his servant?"

"Ah. Good question. She had no ties to him. Unlike Mammon, greed does not drive her. He could not bond with her. With any of the *Justitians* over the years. And his servant, or—" He clears his throat. "—gnome-like creature, as you called them, never cared for him like my"—he pronounces the name of my *justitia*, a name unpronounceable for human lips—"cared for me. It would never have worked. His plan was doomed from the start. Only I prevailed. Only I will rule. And you will rule by my side."

I don't think so, buster. "Like hell I will."

"Yes, that is what I said. You will like Hell."

"You misunderstand. There is no way ever I will go with you. Set me free, Zagan. You don't really want me. You want the entity in here," I hold up my wrist with the *justitia*. "The one you loved. Set me free and we'll leave you alone. I'll make sure the Agency will leave you alone. They already think you're dead."

His eyes narrow. His mouth opens as his hand reaches for me. I try to move but my feet won't cooperate. Fear hollows my insides to ice.

A bolt of lightning flashes through the air, missing Zagan only because he jumps out of the way. A pissed off Smythe strides through the cemetery gate, energy hovering above his palm in a swirling ball of blue light.

"Get away from her, Zagan. She's mine, not yours."

Zagan plants his feet, a glowing mass of red in his upturned palm. A snarl morphs his face into a mask of fury. "She belonged to me for longer than you've known her. That makes her mine."

When I was younger, I thought it would be cool if two guys fought over me. In reality, having two guys pull magic into the form of glowing energy balls was damn scary. Not cool at all.

Although words can't describe how happy I am to see Smythe defending my frozen self from the big, bad demon.

"Let her go. We've helped you ascend to the throne of Hell. The least you can do is set her free."

"She belongs to me." Zagan pitches his red energy

ball at Smythe, who dodges the flaming orb. It slams into a headstone, knocking the ancient marker over.

Ouch. This place might give me the creeps but seeing it damaged hurt. Ancient sites shouldn't be destroyed.

Smythe lobs an energy ball at Zagan. Who dodges the thing. Released from whatever spell held them frozen to the ground, my feet move when I try to run. Finally! I duck behind a tall obelisk in the middle of the graveyard. Since my *justitia* refuses to turn into a sword, I'm useless in this fight.

Unlike Smythe. While Zagan continues dodging a round of energy balls thrown at him, my mage speaks a spell thickening the air. A warding spell to keep out prying eyes?

Nope. Not that. Judging by Zagan's wide-eyed expression whatever Smythe speaks affects him. And not in a good way. The demon forms a hurried portal, vanishing inside its depths as a blast of energy shoots from Smythe's hands.

Master gone. The longing tone in the *justitia's* voice grates on my nerves.

If you love him, why do you call him Master?

Silence greets my question. Why am I not surprised? Just as well, I'm not sure I want to carry on a conversation with the thing at the moment.

"Gin! Get your ass over here now!"

Smythe's bellow snaps me upright. He's never spoken to me in that tone of voice. Sure, he's been beyond pissed at me, but I can't recall a time he's told me to get my ass over there.

Which means I do as he says posthaste. He grabs my arm, speaks his portal forming words and transports us to the door of the Agency before I have time to draw in a breath. After speaking the unlocking spell, he yanks the door open, ushers me inside, and slams it shut. A few more words and the door disappears, smoothing into a wall.

My breath saws in and out of my lungs as if I ran for miles. Or had the bejeezus scared out of me. Or maybe faced an irate mage.

Okay. I can't blame him for being mad at me. I'm a little mad at myself. Not that I'd admit it. I'd rather thank him for getting me out of a cluster.

"Thank you."

"Jesus H. Christ, Gin. What the fuck were you thinking?" His fingers flex and release as he glares at me.

I swallow, forcing my feet to stay in place. "How did you know?"

"What the fuck were you thinking?" He draws in a deep breath through his nose, a fine tremor of anger and fear shaking his limbs. "I knew you were up to something, so I followed you. He almost had you. Almost took you away from me. Jesus, Gin, if I hadn't followed, you'd be as good as dead."

I swallow, fixing my gaze on my feet. Smythe is right. As usual. I shouldn't have gone to Zagan. Then again, the demon has been trustworthy in his dealings with me.

I give myself a mental smack. The demon of deceit trustworthy? Clearly I'm not thinking straight. Then again, when it comes to Zagan, have I ever?

"I'm sorry. He wanted to talk, and I didn't realize taking me to Hell was on his agenda. I wanted to convince him to remove his mark. To set me free." I shake my head as I look Smythe in the eye. "It didn't work out as I hoped."

"As I've said before, he's a fucking demon. He can't be trusted."

"And yet we agreed to help him."

"You agreed. We were hunting Mammon anyway." He huffs. "As much as I hate to admit it, him giving you the ability to use his energy helped win the fight."

"Zagan's not all bad." Kidnapping attempt aside. "But I do want this mark removed." I point to my neck, as if Smythe needs a reminder.

He runs a hand through his hair. "Working on it."

I step to him, place my hand on his chest, feel his heart racing beneath the pads of my fingers. "Thank you. I didn't mean for you to have to come get me. I thought I could handle him on my own. I always had before."

His arms wrap around me, draw me close, as he rests his head on top of mine. "When I saw him gather energy to whisk you away…I about lost it."

"Looked to me like you had things under control. Whatever spell you cast there at the end had him running."

He pulls back a little so he looks down at me, a grin turning his lips. "Yeah, it did. I've been doing research on him and learned an ancient spell to render him immobile until he agrees to my terms." His grin vanishes as his face hardens. "But he escaped."

"Wait a minute." I pull away to look him in the eyes. "You mean you figured out a way to get him to release me from his mark?"

"I hope. I'm working on it. That spell I found is the only thing coming to mind. There isn't anything about a demon releasing a human from servitude—"

"I'm not his servant." I am not. I'd know it if I was, right? Right.

Judging from his brow-cocked expression, Smythe doesn't believe me.

"Mmm. I need to get back." Slinging an arm over my shoulders, he heads toward the elevator at the end of the hall.

"I'm not his servant." I have a need to make sure he realizes the truth behind my words. "If I was, I wouldn't have fought him."

"You didn't fight him. Your *justitia* remained a bracelet."

"I've told you before, it thinks of Zagan as a friend." Or lover, but I refuse to touch that pile of unwanted knowledge with a ten-foot pole.

"Mmm." He shoves the UP button to call the elevator. "I'll take you back to the apartment."

"I'm not sleepy."

"I need you to be someplace where I won't worry about you. And my apartment would be it. Okay?"

A flash of anger slams into me. He speaks to me like I'm a child. Then again, I lied to him about where I was going, caused him to have to rescue me, and almost gave both of us heart attacks.

"The apartment it is."

He nods, his arm tightening around my shoulders. "I don't want to lose you."

"I'm not going anywhere. Except to your apartment."

True to his word, he drops me off at his apartment with a quick kiss before heading off for another round of question-the-evil-mages. T is nowhere to be found.

T? Where are you?

A long pause, then his voice pops into my mind, exasperation running through the tone. *Please tell me you aren't in trouble.*

Nope. Back at Smythe's. Thought you might want to watch TV?

I'm busy. Talk to you later.

He terminates our mental bond. What...oh. Never mind. I get it. Heat slaps my cheeks. Busy is a euphemism. I guess Eloise took a break from questioning mages.

I click on the TV, flipping through the channels until I reach a home network channel with happy people looking for houses in different countries.

Sounds good. A great accompaniment to the thoughts racing through my head.

Why did I trust Zagan not to try to steal me away? How stupid was I? Instead of demeaning self talk, I need to discover a way to escape him once and for all. Yes, he's helped me throughout my life. Yes, he's been with me since I was young, but still. Some relationships need to end. Sooner rather than later.

Chapter Twenty-Three

A ringing phone snaps me out of sleep. I blink in confusion. The phone rings again and I glance toward the sound. My phone sits on the coffee table in Smythe's apartment. I remember now. I must've fallen asleep in front of the TV.

I grab the phone, swipe on the call button, and hold it against my ear. "Hello?"

"Took you long enough to pick up." Tiredness laces Smythe's voice.

"Good morning to you, too. Wait. Is it morning?" A quick glance at the window shows light brushing against the shades. Definitely morning. "Why didn't you come home?"

He yawns. "Got busy questioning the mages. I'll sleep later. The higher ups called a meeting."

"I thought the higher ups were dead. No offense." Heat splashes my cheeks. "I'm sorry about your dad."

He pauses. "Yeah. I'm sorry he was persuaded to follow Mammon. I don't want to talk about him right now. As I said, the higher ups called a meeting with all the mages not influenced by Mammon and requested your presence. It's in thirty minutes in the briefing room. You remember where that is?"

"Maybe."

He gives me the floor and room number. "See you then." The call disconnects before I can tell him yes or no.

Mages. Always thinking they have the right of things.

In all fairness, he's usually correct.

I stand and stretch, vertebrae cracking with a you-slept-wrong tune. Heading toward the bathroom, I try to remember who the higher ups are. Chuck, aka Mammon, was the leader of the Agency. David was the leader of the mages. Who else would there be?

The answer refuses to come to me. By the time I make it to the briefing room with my extra-large coffee mug in hand, I'm still confused. Smythe leans against the wall by the door, ankles and arms crossed, his chin halfway to his chest.

My poor guy. He must be exhausted. His eyes open as I step closer. I give him a peck on the cheek. He gives me a hug as he straightens.

"You look tired."

"I am tired. Ready for the meeting?"

"Only if you tell me who the higher ups are. I don't remember anyone else other than your dad and Chuck."

A grin tugs the corners of his lips. "VPs. They worked with Chuck, I mean Mammon, but weren't swayed by him. They're clean. Embarrassed they didn't realize what he was, but clean. James McMillan and Nancy Swayze."

"I don't recall them being at the meeting where the minions attacked."

"They don't like stage attention. They were there. Just not up front."

I nod. Okay, then. Question answered.

"Ready?" Smythe grabs the golden doorknob.

I nod, following him inside. A group of people

crowd into the room, half of them standing against the walls. I see the cleanup crew who helped at my house and offer them a grin. Since they are here, I assume they weren't influenced by Mammon. Nice to know they were some of the good mages. Smythe pauses as he glances around with wide-eyes.

"I'm sorry. I thought the meeting started now."

A thin, balding man seated at the head of the table stands. "It does. We gathered early to discuss another issue."

Smythe stiffens. I grab his hand, give it a squeeze. Unlike usual when we touch, where his thoughts are a pleasant blank slate, his emotions slam into my mind. Fear and resolution swirl together in a heart-pounding mix.

He's afraid they're going to blame him for David's duplicity.

A brief squeeze and he drops my hand, planting his feet and straightening his spine. "What issue?"

The man glances to the dark-brown-skinned woman sitting next to him. She stands.

"Aidan. Before we get to the issue, we would like to extend Gin thanks for her role in killing Chuck, or should I say Mammon. Gin, you have proven yourself a force to be reckoned with and we are grateful to have you on our team."

My cheeks heat as applause breaks out. Wow. I never thought to hear those words from someone at the Agency. It feels nice.

"Thank you." I nod, grinning like a fool until the clapping fades.

Nancy speaks as all eyes turn to Smythe. "In regard to the issue James mentioned, Aidan. We were discussing all that you've done for us over the last couple of days. Without your help, we would never have discovered Chuck was a demon in our midst. We would still be under his thrall. Unfortunately, so many of us believed and followed the demon willingly. Even if they didn't know he was a demon, they are still guilty for he did many illegal things in direct violation of Agency policies.

"Our fellow mages went along with these policies. Policies leading to the death of *Justitians.* Policies where they willingly sold their souls to the devil himself. Trust in our fellow mages is at an all-time low. Those in this room are the only ones trustworthy and we have discussed filling our empty positions. James," she nods at the man standing next to her, "will become the leader of the Agency, while I will remain in my usual role. We have voted and would like you to take over for your father."

Smythe freezes, not even his chest moves. Then he blinks several times. Clears his throat. Swallows. Draws in a breath.

"Come again?"

"We would like for you to accept the position as the leader of the mages."

"Even knowing my father betrayed the Agency by following Mammon?"

"We have looked into your mind and saw you knew nothing about your father's betrayal. You are innocent of his sins. What say you? Do you accept?"

Everyone in the room stares at Smythe, watches as he blinks and swallows. I don't have to touch him to know his emotions. Relief and surprise war for dominance. I know he wants the position and believes he's strong enough to lead. But a small part of him needs to prove to the mage world he can lead, prove he can be in charge, if only to assuage the guilt he feels regarding his ex-girlfriend's death.

A smile breaks across his lips, spreading across his face as he nods. "I accept. On one condition."

"What is that?" Nancy asks.

"Things will change. I discovered financial transactions of Chuck's, I mean Mammon's, that need to stop. We at the Agency cannot go on as we have."

"Agreed. The three of us," she gestures to James, "will lead the Agency into greatness."

A slow beat growing faster and faster spreads across the room as the mages begin to clap. I join in, happy for Smythe, but uncertain what it means for our relationship.

How can he continue as my guardian mage if he is the leader of the mages? Won't he have to remain here while I fight demons around the world? More like in the USA, but still. He'll be here, and I'll be in Texas.

Provided I keep my job. And build or buy a new house. And what will I do before that happens? Live here? Portal to work? Will I remain a nurse? What else would I do to bring in money?

Plastering a smile on my face, I try to be happy for Smythe. Because I'm really happy for him. Really. I am. It's me with the uncertain future. Not him.

Life changing moments always produce an equal mixture of joy and sadness as one struggles with what the future holds.

People come to congratulate Smythe, shove their way between him and me, furthering the imaginary divide between us. I step to the side until the wall stops my progress.

No one pays me and my pity party any attention.

Which is probably a good thing. Smythe deserves the limelight, not me.

Actually, Eloise deserves the limelight. Without her, nothing would have changed. Although something tells me she wants to remain as inconspicuous as possible regarding her role in tracking Mammon. Mum's the word on her involvement.

Instead I watch as Smythe garners much deserved praise. He deserves this, deserves each and every accolade, and so much more.

So why do I feel like our relationship will never be the same?

Chapter Twenty-Four

Once enough of the mages left for Smythe to notice I'm no longer beside him, he motions me over. I shove off the wall, force a smile on my face, and walk to his side. He wraps an arm around my shoulders.

"Gin and her brother killed Mammon."

James and Nancy nod at his announcement, no surprise at all on their faces. Either they already knew about T's role or they're the best actors in the world.

Nancy pats Smythe's free arm. "You're dead on your feet. Why don't you get some rest? We'll continue questioning the followers and let you know the results."

Smythe nods. "Yeah. Maybe you're right."

Of course she's right. I don't need my nursing license to realize he's half asleep and thoroughly exhausted.

"It was nice meeting you, James and Nancy." A smile turns my lips as I shake their hands.

And get an empathic reading. Always good to know one's coworkers.

Both exude confidence and concern, totally appropriate for the situation. No obscure emotions darkened by a demon's touch.

I'm going to enjoy working with them.

"Nice to finally meet you too, Gin." Nancy says while Jim nods in agreement.

"When I wake, we can discuss plans for the

Agency." Smythe gives them a half-wave as he directs me to the door, not bothering for their response.

As soon as the door shuts behind us, I lean my head on his shoulder, giving his waist a squeeze. "Congrats, oh mage leader."

"Thanks. Not at all what I expected."

"I know. But you'll be good at it."

"I hope." He pinches the top of his nose. "I have ideas, but no clue how to implement them."

"Don't worry about it now. You'll figure it out." I punch the UP button on the elevator. "Nancy's right. You need to rest. You look pooped."

The doors to the elevator slide open and we step inside. Smythe pushes the button to his floor. As the doors close, he drops his arm from my shoulders and leans against the wall.

"Yeah. I am."

"Well, we can fix that right now. One bed and snooze session coming up."

He grins and shuts his eyes. When the elevator arrives on his floor, I wrap my arm around his waist, not convinced he can walk without falling. On the other hand, he'd probably take me with him as he fell.

It's the thought that counts.

Once inside his apartment, he makes a beeline to his bedroom, pausing as he gets to the doorway to glance over his shoulder.

"You coming?"

"To sleep?"

"I'm not up for anything else."

I swallow the laugh trying to escape at his unintentional pun and follow him into the bedroom.

****

By the time we wake, night has fallen. According to my phone, it's seven in the evening. A whole day wasted. I turn, watching Smythe stretch. On second thought, a whole day in bed with my guy is not a wasted day.

"Hey."

He blinks a couple of times as a grin spreads across his face. "Hey."

I reach for him, but he rolls the other way, standing and stretching. No hanky-panky for me. Just as well. We have things to discuss.

You know, like demon interference, the fact said demon thinks his mark on my neck means I'm his servant, and Smythe's promotion and what that means for us.

Good times.

Not to mention my breath could conquer a dragon. Mouthwash to the rescue. Thank goodness for a minty-fresh breath solution.

I finish dressing and make my way to the kitchen where Smythe has a pot of coffee brewing. Yeah, it's night, but my body thinks it's morning. And I need all circuits firing to discuss the many things clamoring for a decision.

Smythe hands me a cup of the liquid gold, waiting until I'm halfway through it before talking. He knows me well.

"More important than me taking over leadership of the mages is getting you free of Zagan."

Good point. I'm in total agreement. "That's what I was trying to do last night."

He raises a brow. "Your connection with that demon needs to end."

Despite his point, a need to defend Zagan washes over me. "He can be helpful, you know."

"Yeah." Smythe shakes his head. "His help is finished."

"We agreed to help him win Hell and in return he'd keep most demons in Hell so we don't have to fight them as much." I'm beginning to sound like a whining kindergartener caught in a lie.

"I can't believe you fell for his lie. Do you really think he's going to keep demons away from Earth?"

I bury my response behind a large, tongue burning gulp.

Zagan tell truth. My *justitia* whispers in my mind.

I choke. *You used his name instead of calling him master.*

We equal. Me use his name. The thing huffs like I'm ignorant and retreats from my consciousness.

Okay then. Back to Smythe and my lack of understanding demons.

"I shouldn't have met him without telling you where I was going, but he usually appears after I kill a demon and nothing bad happens, so I assumed nothing bad would happen last night. How was I supposed to know he'd decide to haul my ass to Hell? Thank you again for saving me."

A look of resignation crosses his face. Great. Apparently he thinks it's his lot in life to save my ignorant self from death and destruction. I'm not sure what that says about our relationship.

Yet another topic of discussion.

Narrowed blue eyes focus a bit too long on me, until heat rises in my cheeks. Must be the coffee.

I swallow. "All right. So I made a mistake." He

raises a brow. "Okay, a big-ass mistake. I'm sorry. I'm glad you are there for me when I make stupid mistakes. I'm working on getting better. It would help if I didn't have a demon trying to turn me into his servant."

"Trying?" He slashes a hand through the air. "Never mind. We need to get you away from him. For good. That spell I tried to cast last night is supposed to immobilize him until he gives us what we want."

A knock on the door interrupts our conversation. Smythe gives the door a curious look before hurrying to open it. Eloise and T enter. After setting down my mug, I give them hugs.

"What brings you here this early?" At their what the heck expressions, I shake my head. "Sorry. We slept all day so it's early for us."

T pats me on the shoulder while shaking his head. "Early evening, you mean."

"Whatever. You know what I'm trying to say."

"We wanted to congratulate Aidan on his promotion." Eloise turns to Smythe, opening her arms for a hug.

"Yeah, congrats." T thumps him on the back. "Way to go."

"Thanks." Smythe grins. "Have a seat, maybe you can help."

After everyone sits on the couch declining coffee— for some reason none of them wanted caffeine this late—Smythe loops them into our conversation.

"We're discussing how to get Gin away from Zagan. He tried to kidnap her last night, to take her with him to Hell. I've found a spell to immobilize him until he gives us what we want but he escaped before I could finish casting it."

"I'll help you with the spell." Eloise leans forward, a gleam in her eyes. "I think I know the one you mean."

Chapter Twenty-Five

Two hours later we have our plan in place. I call Zagan, leaving a message for him to meet me at the same cemetery under the guise of wanting another chance to hear his offer.

It's not a lie. I do want to hear it again, so we can cast an ancient spell on him to force him to grant our wishes. Hopefully he'll get the message and run to meet me without realizing it's a trap.

Fingers and toes crossed the spell works.

Burning in Hell is not on my to-do list.

In case Zagan has spies watching me, Eloise portals T and Smythe to a block away from the cemetery, while I walk. Like last night, pedestrians and bar hoppers crowd the street. A cool breeze filled with the scent of fried food and ocean chills me and I shove my hands deeper into the pockets of the jacket Smythe gave me.

One he clearly bought for me and kept in his apartment since it fits me and would be too small on him. Yet another way he shows he cares for me.

Maybe I'm making too big of a deal about his promotion interfering with our relationship. Once we finish with Zagan I'll talk to Smythe. See how he feels about us.

I hate those types of conversations. Although I've got to be honest, I'd rather have a relationship conversation than remain Zagan's supposed servant. At least after tonight there will be no doubt in Smythe's mind I'm not the demon's servant.

Provided the spell works. It will. It has to.

Positive thoughts, Gin, positive thoughts.

The crowd thins the closer I get to the cemetery as if they are afraid of being close to the spirits' haunting grounds. When I arrive, the gate is unlocked, taking the B out of what I thought would be a B&E. Unlike last night, I'm not sure Zagan is here. My *justitia* remains quiet, not its usual happy dance in the demon's presence. So if Zagan didn't unlock the gate, who did?

Duh, Gin. Find your brain. Clearly Smythe, T and Eloise got here first, ensuring the gate was opened.

Sometimes I wonder about myself. Not an insight I want when about to face a demon who thinks I belong to him.

Shadows dance across upright and toppled gravestones as branches creak in the wind. I don't see the others, which is the point.

We're here. Smythe's voice drifts into my mind.

I don't see—my thought trails off as my *justitia* rattles a happy dance. *Wait. He's here. Gotta go.*

I throw mental barriers around my mind, not needing the distraction of a conversation. My brain needs to be on high alert to avoid another kidnapping attempt.

"Zagan. I know you're here."

Zagan materializes in front of a grave as if he'd been there all along, cloaked in an illusion. I swallow, wanting to huddle in my jacket, to shake the chill running down my spine.

Instead, I step forward, hold my head high and

hope I can speak past my dry throat.

"Ah, Gin. You've decided to come with me and rule Hell by my side?"

"Tempting, but no. I want you to set me free."

He chuckles. "No. You are too valuable."

I roll my eyes, mouth opening on a comeback. Only to freeze as a purple light flares inside me, the entity along my nerves taking control of my body.

Oh shit.

But instead of walking me to the demon, the entity uses my mouth to speak in Demonese, an ancient demonic language I would normally find impossible to pronounce. Heavy words twist on my tongue and lips, unfamiliar but nonetheless, I know what I'm saying.

"Set me free."

Zagan's eyes pop wide. "Flower?"

Wait a minute. The name of my *justitia*, a name I can't normally pronounce, translates to flower? I want to laugh, but since the entity, ahem, I mean Flower, controls my lips my chuckle stays firmly in my head.

"This vessel suits me. And Gin is not made for hellfire. She would die. Make good on her wish and set her free."

"But—"

"No buts. She is not yours."

"Ah, but she is. I have known her for years."

"That may be true, but she is not yours. Knowing a human does not give you possession over them."

"You would choose her over me?"

"It is not a choice. If I wish to live I must stay with her. She cannot go with you and live. I cannot allow you to take her."

Zagan glares at me for a second as he paces in a

zigzag pattern to avoid gravestones.

"I don't like it."

Flower remains mute, letting him think things through. While he thinks, I try to locate my friends and brother. They stand at the corners of the cemetery, minds closed, bodies frozen. Did Zagan freeze them, or are they waiting until he tries to grab me before making a move?

He stops in front of me, his warm breath fanning across my face. "I don't like it, but I appreciate you giving your life for me. Even if the end result was not what I intended, you freely gave yourself for my plans. I will grant you your wish."

He places his hands on my cheeks and inside my body I shiver, waiting for his touch to hemorrhage my brain. Except nothing happens. I can't even get a read on his emotions, emotions that normally strike me as evil tangles. Best guess is that being possessed by the entity, Flower, in my *justitia* mutes my empathic abilities.

Good thing too. The last time Zagan touched me skin on skin my brain almost exploded.

He leans forward, his lips brushing against mine, his fingers stroking my throat. A white-hot jolt zips through my body as we kiss. This time he keeps his tongue to himself, thank god.

When he pulls away, I know his mark no longer rests on my neck.

"Your host is free." His voice holds a tone of resignation, a clue he'd rather have kept me for himself.

"Thank you."

Zagan smiles at Flower's words, as the purple light inside me disappears, allowing me control over my limbs. I stumble back.

"You freed me."

"Against my wishes." He steps toward me, only to freeze as Smythe and Eloise hit him with a spell.

What the heck? They let him kiss me with no problem but when he tries to say good-bye they get upset?

Anger flares in his black eyes as Smythe and Eloise walk toward us, speaking the spell. I wave a hand at them.

"It's okay, he's already freed me."

They continue walking forward and casting the spell as if I hadn't spoken. When they finish, Zagan stands with immobilized limbs, his glare strong enough to send me stepping backward.

"I set her free."

Smythe ignores Zagan as he strides to my side. He pulls my hair away from my neck, creates a small light in his palm, and peers at where Zagan's mark used to be.

"You're right." He drops my hair, giving my shoulder a squeeze before walking to Zagan. "We didn't see you cast the spell to free Gin. Why not?"

Zagan's glare could heat the Arctic. But he answers. After a long pause. "I sensed you both and froze you."

"Makes sense." Smythe nods. "Time shifted as soon as you arrived. Since we didn't see you remove her mark—"

Thank god he missed seeing Zagan kiss me. Small favors.

"—we thought you were trying to take her again."

"Now that we have that settled, unfreeze me. Gin is

no longer mine." Zagan growls the words, clearly unhappy with this turn of events.

Too bad. I want to shout 'I'm free, I'm free' but refrain. Now is not the time.

Smythe nods, but before he can release the demon, a request pops into my mind.

"Wait!" All eyes turn to me. "What's the spell to create more *justitias*?"

Zagan barks a laugh. "I am sorry to say they cannot be created. You need demons and unwilling humans. Now release me."

An idea blossoms. "Okay, what about a release mechanism so they can be passed to others not in a family line?"

His lips press together. "If I tell you"—he turns to Smythe—"you promise to release me?"

"We do swear," Eloise answers.

"We do swear," Smythe echoes.

"Very well." He tells them the spell. "Now release me."

After a quick glance at each other, Smythe and Eloise free him. He shakes his arms, his legs. Grins at me. A shiver shakes my spine as he speaks.

"Au revoir." He winks, as his grin widens. "Be happy. Thank you for your help winning Hell." He bows. "My debt to you is complete."

A portal forms above him, swallowing him before I can ask why he's decided to say good-bye in French instead of English. An answer I can live without.

I'm free. Free of the demon of deceit. Free of the uncertainty of whether or not I was truly his servant.

I miss him already. But only a little.

Gah. I might be free, but I still have issues.

Thank you for fighting for me.

Flower preens. *Me like you. You make me happy. Me stay with you.*

I like you too. Thank you.

Talk to mage. She disappears into my mind.

Smythe stands in front of me, a smile turning his lips. "You did it."

"My *justitia* did it. She argued for my freedom."

T wraps his arms around me.

"Where were you?"

He points to a corner of the graveyard. "Over there. Wasn't frozen like Smythe and Eloise but didn't want to give myself away. In case I needed to call the ghosts."

"I'm free of him."

"I heard."

Eloise steps beside him, patting my arm. "Glad he released you without a fight."

"Thank you for coming."

"Want to walk around?" Smythe gestures to the street. "We can walk back to the Agency. I'll show you some of the sights."

"You mean you'll show me the bar scene." I grin.

"Same thing."

"There's too much history here for it to be the same thing."

He shrugs. "Come on. The night is young."

Sure it is. But I follow him away from the cemetery and watch as he locks the gate behind us.

After a couple of hours of walking around in the cold and ducking into a bar for a beer, Eloise portals us to Smythe's apartment.

T and Eloise head to her apartment, leaving us

alone to discuss our next moves in our relationship. Still on a freedom high, the thought of our upcoming discussion doesn't bother me as much as it had earlier.

Smythe sits on the couch, pats the cushion next to him. "You look like you have something on your mind."

"How did you know?" I sit beside him, rubbing my thumb along the pads of my fingers.

"You should be happier. You escaped being a demon's servant. Probably the first person to do so. And yet, you look like someone stole your favorite toy."

I draw in a deep breath. "With your promotion, what's going to happen to us?"

His brow furrows. "Whatcha mean? You no longer want to be together because I got a promotion?"

"Hell no! I mean, will you still be my guardian? How will that work if I'm out fighting and you are here doing the mage leader thing?"

Relief flows into his expression. "Simple. You move here."

"I need my job."

"No, you don't. If you want to work in the infirmary as a nurse, you can, but I'm changing things. We can pay the *Justitians*. Most of them live at Agencies around the world, but they don't get paid. And they should. They put their lives on the line every day. You could stay here with me and help get things set up."

My mouth opens and closes. The opportunity he gave me had never crossed my mind. But I liked it.

"You'll pay me? What about Will? Would you pay him too to train as a mage?"

"Yep. We need all the help we can get." One corner of his lips kicks up. "Good thinking on the spell you requested from Zagan. We might not be able to replicate the bracelets, but we can share them with more women. We no longer need to wait until a *Justitian* dies to pass on the bracelet and if an ancestral line dies out, it won't be a problem."

"Except for me." I glance to the silver links surrounding my wrist. "I don't want to part with Flower."

"Flower?"

"That's her name." I move my wrist back and forth. "I can't pronounce it in Demonese but it translates to Flower."

"How... never mind." He shakes his head. "So you'll do it? You'll stay here with me and work full time for us?"

A grin turns my lips. I don't even have to think hard about it. The thought of not working at Blue Forest Emergency Department no longer sends a jolt of fear tearing through my veins. "Yes. I accept your offer."

He stands, holding out his hand. "Want to seal the offer with a kiss? Or something more?"

My grin spreads as I take his hand, as he pulls me to my feet. "Sure thing, Boss."

He kisses me, firm lips pressing against mine, pulling away too soon. "Come on."

Taking my hand, he leads me to his bedroom.

A feeling of lightness makes my feet feel like they float on the air. I'm free. Free of my past. Free of my demon. Free of the fear binding me for so long.

But the best thing isn't the sense of relief flowing through my veins. The best thing, the truly greatest thing, to come out of all this mess is the one thing I first believed horrid: meeting Aidan Smythe.

As he kicks his bedroom door closed and pulls me into his embrace, I know despite the horrible things in my past, my future with this man shines like a beacon of comfort.

And I am now at peace.

A word about the author...

Karilyn Bentley's love of reading stories—and preference of sitting in front of a computer at home instead of in a cube—drove her to pen her own works, blending fantasy and romance mixed with a touch of funny.

Her paranormal romance novella *Werewolves in London* placed in the Got Wolf contest and started her writing career as an author of sexy heroes and lush fantasy worlds.

Karilyn lives in Colorado with her own hunky hero, a crazy dog aka The Kraken, a funny puppy known as Sir Barks-A-Lot, and a handful of colorful saltwater fish.

Find out more about Karilyn at:
www.karilynbentley.com

www.ingramcontent.com/pod-product-compliance
Lightning Source LLC
Chambersburg PA
CBHW060534260626
47161CB00003B/890

* 9 7 8 1 5 0 9 2 2 5 2 6 2 *